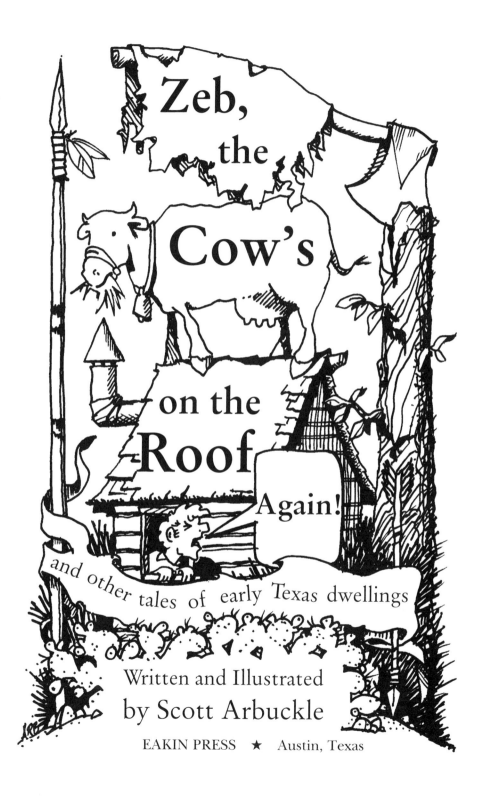

Zeb, the Cow's on the Roof Again!

and other tales of early Texas dwellings

Written and Illustrated by Scott Arbuckle

EAKIN PRESS ★ Austin, Texas

Library of Congress Cataloging-in-Publication Data

Arbuckle, Scott.
    Zeb, the cow's on the roof again : and other tales of early Texas dwellings / by Scott Arbuckle.
        p.   cm.
    Summary: A collection of stories introducing the dwellings of some early Texas inhabitants, including the Coman che tipi, the settlers' dugouts and dog-trots, and the Greek Revival mansion of the Civil War period.
    ISBN 1-57168-102-7
    1. Dwellings—Texas—Juvenile fiction. 2. Frontier and pioneer life—Texas—Juvenile fiction. 3. Texas—Juvenile fiction. 4. Children's stories, American.   [1. Dwellings—Texas—Fiction. 2. Frontier and pioneer life—Texas—Fiction. 3. Texas—Fiction. 4. Short stories.]
    I. Title.
    PZ7.A6743Ze   1996
    [Fic]—dc20
                                                                                96-8489
                                                                                CIP
                                                                                AC

To Tammy – my wife,
my companion, my patient typist

Contents

Who Lived Here?   vi

Coati's Mistake   1
    Chapter 1   Old Quatl   3
    Chapter 2   Burning Tipi   6
    Chapter 3   The Great Hunt   10
    Chapter 4   Kidnapped   15
    Chapter 5   Hard Work!   23
    Chapter 6   The Last Chance   27
    About the Comanche Tipi   34

The Sod-House   35
    Chapter 1   Daddy's Dying   37
    Chapter 2   Diggin' into A Surprise   42
    Chapter 3   Sod-Stackin'   46
    Chapter 4   There's a Reason for That Fence   51
    Chapter 5   Soddie, Sweet Soddie   62
    About the Settler's Dugout of the 1800s   66

From Dog-Trot to Mansion   **67**

   Chapter 1   Frontier Architect   69

   Chapter 2   A Mansion for the Kerns   73

   Chapter 3   The Party   79

   Chapter 4   Stuck in a Dog-Trot   89

   About the Dog-Trot and Plantation Mansion   98

Crazy Water City   **99**

   Chapter 1   Dirt Balls   101

   Chapter 2   Camping at Dr. Zeke's   107

   Chapter 3   The Big Hotel   111

   Chapter 4   Swingers   115

   About Architecture of the 1930s   128

Who Lived Here?

The stories in this book were created with the idea that every building has a story to tell, a story of its builders and inhabitants. This is particularly true of houses and homes where the builders and the inhabitants were the same people.

Studying the buildings in which they lived gives us a great look at the early Texans. Whether we're discussing the Native Americans or the Europeans who came later, their homes reveal a great deal to us. Their homes were always a product of the tools they carried in their hands, and the thoughts they carried in their heads.

Architecture is such a useful tool for understanding history because it always answers three important questions about the people who produced it:

1. What did they have?
2. How did they see themselves?
3. Where did they think they were headed?

These three questions outline the approach that I took in writing this book about early Texans and the homes they built.

The first story is about the Comanches and their ingenious High Plains tipi. The main character in this story is Coati (Ko-wah-tee). She is a twelve-year-old girl given the task of building her first tipi. In Comanche society, the tipi was built by, and belonged to, the women of the family.

The second and third stories are about the Anglo settlers who came to Texas in the 1800s. The first shelters these settlers built were primitive by anyone's standards. In West Texas, they built houses of dirt called "soddies," and in East Texas they built "dog-trot" cabins. The fact that these people left safe, comfortable homes elsewhere to live dangerous and difficult lives in Texas tells us they were risk-takers, if nothing else.

The grand southern plantation house is discussed in the third story. This type of house has symbolized many things to many people. One thing that it tells us for sure is that by the 1860s some Texans were no longer struggling to survive. The battle against the wilderness was being won in style.

The fourth story concerns Texans from more recent days. I wanted to write about cities, because that's where most Texans live today. The question has to be asked, "How did Texans go from being mostly country folks to mostly city folks?" To explore that question I created a character who is a disabled farm girl during the Great Depression (in the 1930s). She becomes a city dweller when her family has to flee the Dust Bowl looking for work. Like all of my characters, she's fictional, but she could have been real and not uncommon in her day. She, like so many other Texans before her, shows the great ability to adapt and change, to survive and thrive.

Fascinating people, these Texans. In the stories that follow you'll find out just how fascinating they have been by visiting the homes in which they lived.

Coati's Mistake

Chapter 1

Old Quatl

Hot, white sparks escaped from the top of the council tipi and fluttered into the black night sky. To me, the sparks are like little birds escaping these plains to become stars in the sky. But that is part of my problem. I am often told I spend too much time dreaming silly dreams and not enough time working hard like one of the squaws.

I guess that I am not a very good Comanche. Instead of doing my chores, I sneak off to listen in on these great council fires. The warriors gather there to hear the chiefs speak on important things.

There is one chief I like to hear speak more than any other. He is Quatl. He is older than all the others, so he is not allowed to talk much anymore. The younger chiefs all think they are so much smarter. But I think he is wiser than all the rest.

Maybe it is his face. He reminds me of an old tortoise. His face is hard and wrinkled, but his eyes are kind. Quatl often stops to speak to me as I work around our camp. I hoped the others would let him speak now.

I saw his old, bent shadow against the side of the tipi. He was rising to speak.

"You young braves always want to fight, to raid, because your youth thirsts for honor," Quatl began. "Hunting the buffalo is not enough glory for you. But fighting the white man is far different from our fights with the hated Apache. To the white man, fighting is not a game to be played when there is no other work. They are different from the red man. They keep coming and keep coming, and keep fighting and keep fighting. The white man deals in ownership. We deal with what is enough for today. We move too much, always on the hoof. It is not wise for us to gather things to ourselves. We prefer to let the buffalo and the horse be our wealth. The buffalo move themselves. It is much easier that way.

"But this is our weakness. We can protect ourselves, even our families, but we cannot protect the buffalo. And the buffalo cannot protect himself."

"Your words are like the morning music of the birds, Quatl, but men are here to do more than chirp!" sneered one young chief.

"If I were a chirping bird, I would still have more wisdom than the young of this clan," returned Quatl's quavering voice.

"Let him finish, let him finish!" came the impatient voices of the other chiefs.

"Quatl only has this more to say," said Quatl. "You young braves can raid the whites and steal their horses, and bring many scalps back to camp where all the young maids will be impressed. But the game is not over for the whites. As clumsy as they are, they are determined. They will not forget an offense. And if they can't find us to fight, they can always fight our friend the buffalo."

"Fight the buffalo? Why would any man fight the buffalo?" many voices asked.

"Because when the buffalo is gone, our way of life is gone," answered Quatl. "If the white man takes our buffalo, we shall have to learn to eat corn like the Pueblos, the ones our ancestors vanquished from the plains."

For much time no answer came back to Quatl. I could see his stooped shadow return to be seated. Grumbles filled the air, until one young chief stood to speak.

"Old Quatl, your age is a dishonor to you. All Comanches know that the brave die young. Your face is old and your words are not brave. We will drive the whites from these plains just as our fathers drove the Apaches from here. You no longer have a voice at this fire."

I stared at the shadow on the tipi wall that I knew was Quatl's. His tired old form rose and silently left the council fire. I saw him emerge from the tipi's door and disappear into the night.

It is not unusual for old men to slip away from our camp when they feel they no longer have the respect of the tribe. I am told that they live by themselves quietly until they die. But I have always held a special place for old Quatl in my heart. Seeing his bent old body totter out of camp gave me deep sadness.

Chapter 2

Burning Tipi

I slipped back to my tipi. My family was bedding down. Without looking into my mother's eyes, I hopped over my sisters and under my blanket, before she could ask where I had been.

When I sensed that everyone was asleep, I poked my face from under the blanket. The sleeping shapes of all my family members were still and lined up around the campfire. We all lay with our feet toward the fire and our heads pointed to the outside of our circular tent. It reminded me of the white man's wagon wheel. Each of us was one of the spokes.

I looked up through the opening in the top of the tipi where the smoke of the campfire escaped. I could see a few stars through this opening. When I was the only one awake, on nights like this, I had learned to play a little game. Through the buffalo blanket that covered me, I could still nudge a log in the fire, with my foot.

This would always send a swarm of sparks up from the fire and they would flutter through the opening at the top of the tipi. I imagined that I was setting my little glowing friends free. It was a silly game for a girl my age to play. But as I felt sad for Quatl, playing the game seemed to cheer me up.

I kept playing my little game, ever so often nudging the logs and watching the sparks, until I noticed something strange. A funny smell began to fill the tipi. The nice smell of burning wood and buffalo chips was being replaced by a thick, ugly odor. To a Comanche, a new smell often means danger. I sat up, and to my horror, I saw that my father's buffalo blanket was on fire!

In an instant, I realized that I had nudged the fire so much that I had pushed it into my father's bedding! Not only that, but the sparks from both fires had landed on the inside walls of our tipi. The tipi was beginning to burn!

I was frozen in fear. I knew we were in danger, but I knew not what to do. In a panic, I wiggled out of my blanket and madly crawled on top of my brothers and sisters around the tipi to my father's smoldering blanket. I pounded and slapped his legs where the blanket was burning. He, of course, was surprised when he

7

awoke to find his tipi full of smoke and one of his children beating his legs.

Now everyone was awake. Coughing and shouting and smoke filled our tipi. In our rush to find the entrance flap to our tipi, my family managed to push the whole flaming mess over to one side. The entire tipi collapsed on us like a giant smoldering sack. For a moment, I could see nothing. Then a knife ripped through the part of the tipi we were trapped under, and I felt strong arms pulling me free from the collapsed tipi.

Once my smoke-stung eyes quit watering, I could see that the entire tribe seemed to be standing around our smoldering tipi. I quickly counted my brothers and sisters as each was pulled free from the tipi that now lay on its side. Finally, my father and mother crawled free.

I was so relieved to see all of us safe. In fact, the whole tribe was so relieved that a great burst of roaring laughter broke loose. I guess we looked pretty strange. My father looked the strangest. Some of his clothes were charred from the fire, and one of his hair braids had completely burned off. This was not good, because Comanche braves are very proud of their hair.

It was easy for me to see from my father's face that he was very angry and very embarrassed. My face must have shown my guilt, for he knew immediately that I was somehow at fault. My mother, my sisters, my brothers, and the whole village looked on as he strode over to where I stood.

"Coati?" he addressed me in a fierce voice.

"Y-yes?" I stammered as I stared at the ground.

8

"You were playing with the fire again?" he demanded to know.

"Yes, Father," I almost whispered, still afraid to look in his fierce warrior eyes. The whole village was silently waiting to see what would happen next. It seemed they waited for a long time, but finally he spoke again.

"It falls on you, then, to make a new tipi for our family. I want it completed before we break here to go to our winter camp. Do not fail in this!"

With that said, my father turned and walked away from me, and the camp went about returning to sleep. Aunts and uncles gathered up my family to sleep in their tipis. Except for me. I was left standing alone by the smoking remains of our tipi.

I was relieved. It would not have been unusual for a child my age to have been beaten severely for something like this. Mistakes are not taken lightly among Comanches. My punishment was to make a tipi. This was always a squaw's job, but for a twelve-year-old girl like me, making a tipi was going to be a big challenge.

I picked up one of our blankets that had escaped the fire and went to find a grassy place to lie down for the rest of the night.

Chapter 3

The
Great Hunt

The scolding I received the night before was painful for only a few hours. But the punishment my father Wolftail gave me was going to last for a long time. Building a new tipi takes a long time and a lot of work. Sometimes, a single squaw may work on a new tipi for months in between her daily chores. For me, the hardest part would be first getting the twenty or so buffalo hides necessary for one family tipi. If I were a brave, rather than a young girl, it would be easy to go out and kill that many buffalo in a day. But girls like me are too busy with daily cooking and caring for the babies to have time to hunt.

The good news was that it was late summer — time for our entire band to begin the great buffalo hunt for winter meat and hides. Most everything we needed for winter would come from the scores of buffalo killed in the next few days. Meat would be dried, skins tanned, and bones would become tools and weapons. I hoped that a few of the hides would be given to me since everyone knew I needed them for the new tipi. I had to rely on my elders to be generous to me. This was my hope as I lay down to sleep.

The next morning was a joyous time. The entire tribe took part in the buffalo hunt. Every man, woman, and child had a role to fill. It was a celebration of the passing of summer to fall. We would all work hard and eat hearty for the next several days.

The tribe was split into the males, who would do the killing, and the women, who would do the skinning and butchering of the fallen buffalo. As we left the camp, the two groups parted. The hunters took their place near the herd, while we, the butchers, waited in the high grass behind the hunters. The hunters were

mounted on ponies with lances and bows. We were on foot with knives, and the vultures circled overhead. Each group waited on the other.

All was quiet for a moment. The huge herd of brown buffalo stretched out over the grassy plains and under the clear blue sky as far as the eye could see. Heads down, they were eating grass as usual, and waiting for us to feed on them. The buffalo are always there for us.

At the chief's signal the whole scene changed. The quiet morning exploded into the sound of pony hooves and screaming braves. Our men looked like so many bees, attacking a single vast animal. Each bee swooped in and carved out a chunk of the brown mass and left it lying in the late summer grass. Some braves rode their ponies side by side with the buffalo and rammed their lances into the galloping beasts. Other braves preferred the bow, and they knew just where to aim so that a single arrow would bring down a speeding bull.

Buffalo are not terribly smart, so our braves had brought down dozens of the beasts before the herd began to run. We didn't have to wait long. The yellow-green prairie was now dotted with dead buffalo. With one great female voice, we all shrieked with joy and began a foot race to butcher the beasts left behind by the fleeing herd. Into the great cloud of dust stirred up by the herd, each one of us dashed to be the first to reach a carcass.

I tried to follow the aunt who favored me. If I helped her, I hoped she would reward me with a hide or two. She darted from carcass to carcass, looking for one with her man's arrow in it. Once found, she fell to skinning it with vigor. Her knife was slitting the beast from

chin to tail when I pounced on the foreleg and began to work my knife. I grinned at her, and made sure she knew that I was helping. Several of my younger sisters soon joined in the work.

We had the great hide removed from the beast when my uncle rode by and hopped from his pony. His smile was wide and proud as he reclaimed his arrow that we had pulled from the buffalo before the skinning began. My uncle walked up to the skinless carcass and, using his knife, he cut the liver loose. Holding it up proudly, he sank his teeth into the raw organ with great delight. That was usually done to honor the victory of the hunt. Having done with the liver, he cut the carcass into quarters so we could handle them easier. Then he led his pony off to find other carcasses marked with his arrows.

As our work neared completion on the beast, I hoped my aunt would reward my hard work with the great hairy hide. My younger sisters grabbed up armloads of bloody meat, but I went to grab the rolled-up hide, hoping there would be no protest from my aunt. Just as I stooped to gather it up, my aunt shoved me to the ground and pointed to the buffalo's hindquarter. Obviously she had her eye on a new sleeping robe. She gathered the buffalo skin onto her own shoulder to carry back to camp. All I could do was lug the hindquarter she left me.

I was not too discouraged, though. I would help butcher many more buffalo in the next few days. Surely, I thought, one of my elders would give me at least one hide. But again and again, I was disappointed. As each buffalo was divided up, I was left empty-handed.

It seemed that if the young braves showed up to parcel out the meat and hide, they gave the hide to one of the budding maidens just a little older than me. If the older braves were to award the skin, they often gave it to the younger girls, just to laugh at them struggling proudly with their prize. If no men were around to decide, the hide went to the oldest girl. I always seemed to be either too young or too old.

At the end of three days of back-breaking labor, I had no buffalo hides for my tipi and no hope of getting any. The whole tribe celebrated the end of the hunt. But not me. As I lay down to sleep that night, I would have been very troubled had I not been so exhausted. I fell fast asleep.

Chapter 4

Kidnapped

As tired as I was that night, almost nothing could have awakened me. But from my deep slumber I did awake — not from noise, but from two strong hands. One hand circled my waist, and one hand clamped my mouth! My eyes were wide open with terror as I was hoisted noiselessly to someone's shoulder and carried out of the lean-to where my sisters still lay sleeping. In a second, my captor had carried me from the silent, sleeping camp into the dark night.

My mind was racing. An Indian girl's worst fear is being kidnapped by another tribe. It is a common game among braves of all tribes. Only it is no game for the women and girls who are kidnapped. I had seen enough of the treatment of captive girls in our own camp to be terrified of what lay ahead. Sometimes captive girls are taken as wives, but usually they are treated as slaves and abused by the women of the tribe.

Soon my mysterious master gently placed me on the back of a pony and led the pony away. Now I was confused, for this did not seem like a raiding party. There were no other braves, and no haste to escape.

Soon we stopped at a small camp hidden in a cedar break. My captor helped me from the horse and from the first rays of morning I recognized his face.

"Quatl!" I exclaimed.

A slow crease of a smile spread across his ancient face.

"Why have you brought me here?" I asked, not entirely sure I could feel relieved yet.

"I've been watching you. You need an old man's help. I need the sounds of another Comanche."

I looked at the ground. "You saw my family's tipi burn?" I asked.

He just chuckled.

"My father said that I must make a new tipi before winter, but I have no buffalo hides."

The old man said nothing, but he gathered his bow and quiver full of arrows. Then he nodded for me to follow him back out onto the plains.

We waded through the late summer grass that was deep enough to tickle my face. The sun was just beginning to glow on the eastern horizon. The great buffalo herd which had provided my tribe with winter meat still filled the great plain before us.

Quatl motioned for me to stop at a large rock that peeked above the grass. He kneeled down, and then rose dressed in a gray wolf skin. The animal's face hung over Quatl's. I jumped! Fortunately, I did not make enough sound for the herd to notice. Quatl handed a second wolf hide to me, and I pulled it on as he had.

16

Disguised now as wolves, we got on all fours and crawled into the very midst of the buffalo. Trying to maintain a wolf-like appearance, I was afraid to lift my head. But from under the wolf-skin, everywhere I looked were buffalo hooves, and buffalo mouths, nibbling on grass. My hands and knees were caked with fresh buffalo dung. We were so close to the beasts that every snort and bellow seemed to be in my very ear.

I had heard that buffalo had no fear of wolves. Now I saw that it was true. They seemed to care nothing for our presence as we slithered between the beasts' legs. My heart began to pound, though, as I realized that if we spooked the herd, in any way, we would be instantly trampled.

I kept crawling, thinking I was following Quatl, until I blindly bumped into his rump. He had stopped. I peered under the wolf hide to see that Quatl was very slowly pulling arrows from his quiver and putting them to his bowstring. Silently, Quatl began sending arrows into the huge hairy beasts all around us.

I kept count. One arrow flew. One buffalo moaned and fell to the ground! Over and over again, Quatl repeated this trick. Soon there was a wall of fallen buffalo all around us. Yet the herd seemed unbothered. Obviously, the strength of the buffalo is in their great numbers, not their keen minds.

When Quatl quit sending arrows, I had counted twenty buffalo, just the number of hides that I needed for my tipi.

With a solid wall of dead buffalo on all sides of us, Quatl felt safe to stand up and throw off his wolf costume. The herd finally seemed to notice us and shuffled away.

"Come . . . now the real work begins," came his ancient voice. I stood up, and he handed me a knife. We began the large task of skinning twenty dusty buffalo. After we worked for a while, he told me that I should return to the tribe before I was missed.

"I will return when I can," I said, as I tried to be appreciative. He only smiled and kept at his work.

I ran the entire way back to camp. I hoped that I would not be scolded for being late with my morning chores. The camp was still in such a frenzy of celebration, no one seemed to notice me as I tried to blend in to all of the bustling activity of a Comanche camp getting ready for winter.

I worked hard all day fetching water, cutting meat into long strips, and helping to scrape the hides that my aunts and sisters had been lucky enough to claim. I watched closer than I had ever done before, so I would know how to help Quatl when I returned to his camp.

That night, when the camp was settling into resting and visiting, I returned to Quatl. He had the look of a man who had worked hard all day long. He sat in front of a small fire, puffing on his bone pipe. He seemed to smile as I returned. I sat at his feet while I waited for him to finish his pipe. When he finished, he lit a torch and walked a few paces to a flat area where twenty fresh buffalo hides were staked to the ground.

"I made you a scraper," he said proudly. His wrinkled old hand held out a buffalo leg bone. It was clean and smooth and shone in the torchlight. One end was wrapped with rawhide for a handle. The other end was sharpened.

"This will be your friend for many hours," he chuckled. I thanked him and set to work.

With the new tool, I scraped all the blood, meat, fat, and hair from the hides. He was right. My aching hands became all too familiar with that scraper. We worked several nights on our knees, scraping and scraping the twenty hides. As we both worked, Quatl told me many stories. Some were about great fearsome beasts, some about our people. Some I had heard, but many I had not.

In addition to scraping the hides, Quatl had been working during the day preparing the meat for winter. He had cut the buffalo meat into long strips and hung

them to dry on racks of branches. Some of the meat he sent back to camp with me, because it was so much more than he needed. Some of the meat we crushed into pemmican, or powder. He called this "old man's meat" because it did not require chewing to eat.

All of this work was considered squaw work, and I felt sad that Quatl had to live alone and do these things himself. But he seemed happy enough.

Once, while we were both scraping hides by torchlight, he caught me staring at him.

"Are you puzzled to see an old chief doing squaw's work?" he asked with some humor in his voice.

I nodded, a little embarrassed at his question.

"When I was a boy, about your age, I was taken captive by our enemy, the Apache. That was long, long ago. No one left alive in our tribe today would remember this. Instead of killing me, they kept me alive to be a slave. One of the old squaws kept me on a leash. She was one of the Apache chief's wives. I learned to do all of the things that she didn't want to do anymore. I prepared buffalo hides. I cooked. I made clothes. The Apache braves laughed at me a lot."

"How is it that you returned to the Comanches?" I asked.

"One spring morning, the Apaches awoke to find the Comanches raiding their camp. It was our tribe. The entire Apache camp was in turmoil. I cut my leash and ran after my people as they were fleeing with the Apaches' horses. They brought me to my family."

With that, Quatl abruptly ended his story, and I asked no more questions. I felt that I had a better understanding of Quatl and the kindness which he showed me.

Chapter 5

Hard Work!

We continued the scraping and meat preparation for several days. I came to Quatl's camp early in the morning and late in the evening to help. No one at camp ever asked me about my coming and going. I don't know if they knew, or if they really did not notice my absence in a camp as big as ours.

Once the hides were scraped, they had to be tanned. When I came to Quatl's camp one morning, he had piled up two heaps of a yellow greasy goo. One heap was buffalo brains. The other heap was buffalo fat. He said he threw in a few other things too. It smelled awful. All of this had come from the twenty buffalo we had killed the first morning. Everything a Comanche used came from the buffalo. We grabbed handfuls of this stuff and began rubbing it into the scraped buffalo hides.

"This will make them soft and keep them from rotting," explained Quatl. I already knew that. But he seemed to really like teaching me things, so I just listened.

Once this greasy, smelly job was done, Quatl built a small tipi frame over his campfire. We then hung the greasy hides on this framework. Quatl showed me where to cut green, leafy willow branches by the creek near his camp. We threw these by the armload onto the campfire. Big clouds of thick smoke puffed forth from the fire and covered the hides that hung on the racks Quatl built.

"The smoke dries up the grease and makes the hide keep out the rain," the old chief explained.

After the hides were dried out by the smoke, they were a little stiff. So, for several nights, we stretched them back and forth over a tree limb. This softened them. Quatl and I must have looked like we were having a tug-of-war as we jerked each hide back and forth over that limb. First, he would pull his side, nearly pulling me off the ground. Then I would try to pull the hide back to me. With each pull, the hide whistled over the surface of the tree limb.

I knew when this was done that we were getting close to trimming and stitching the hide into a tipi. But I knew that I must still hurry. My father reminded me one day that we would be leaving for our winter camp soon. He said he was expecting my tipi to be complete by then. I did not want to find out what my fate would be if I failed to have the tipi ready. Women in our tribe are expected to do as they are told. Failure to obey is not tolerated.

So far no one in our camp had seen me work on the tipi, so no one expected me to have one ready. They may all have been imagining what my punishment would be. I hoped that I would be surprising them with a new tipi.

With my father's words in my ears, I returned to Quatl's camp eager to see what the next step would be. It was evening, and he was seated by his campfire puffing on his pipe and whittling something with his knife. I drew close to him to see what he was working on.

"It's time to start stitching, so I've made some needles," he said with satisfaction. In his lap were bright, white sewing needles carved from buffalo bones. Lying next to him were coils of buffalo sinew. With the needles, we stitched the hides together with sinew cords into one large covering that would be draped over the tipi poles. The poles had to be straight and true and of the right length. There are very few straight trees on the buffalo plains where we live. But in the small creeks and valleys, cottonwoods and willows grow this way. Finding these long poles is often the hardest part of building a tipi. Twelve to fifteen are needed if you are to have spare poles.

Fortunately, we found the ones we needed in the little canyon that Quatl camped in. The old chief cut them down with his stone-headed axe. Then I stripped off the limbs and bark so the surface would be smooth and would not snag the hides or poke any holes in it.

Finally, the tipi was ready to be put up. First, three of the best poles were laid side by side. Then the three ends on one side were tied together with new rawhide rope. We stood this up and spread the three loose legs out. This frame stood up like a newborn colt. The other poles were stacked against these three to fill out the frame.

I now knew that it was time to drape the giant buffalo hide covering over the framework. I climbed to the top of the poles, pulling part of the covering with me, and hooked it to the top of the poles. The rest of the hide merely draped around the framework. We tied the covering to the bottom of the poles.

After all the days and nights of hard work, scraping the hides, tanning the hides, smoking the hides and stretching the hides, standing up the tipi only took a few moments. Quatl and I stood back and admired the new, yellow-skinned tipi. He then showed me how to adjust the flaps for letting campfire smoke out and how to roll up the sides in the summer.

"One thing left," he announced. "Come back one more night to paint. Also, bring a dog from camp."

"One more night!" I cried. "I hope I have one more night!"

Chapter 6

The Last Chance

As I ran back to camp I thought of how hard I had worked and how far the tipi had come in the days since Quatl snatched me from camp. What a strange adventure! I would be sad to see it end, but relieved to have the work accomplished before my father's displeasure showed again.

As I broke into our camp, my happy thoughts were shattered by what I saw. The chiefs must have decided it was time to move to winter camp. Everywhere I looked people were making ready to move.

The racks that hung with drying buffalo meat had been taken down. Buffalo hides that had been drying and stretching were being rolled up. Water bags were being filled. Mothers were scolding children who were not tending to their tasks. The last thing to be packed were the tribes' tipis. These would be left up until the next morning because a squaw could take one down and pack it up in a matter of minutes.

"Where have you been? We've looked all over camp for you, Coati!" cried my mother. I turned to see her struggling under the load that she was carrying.

"I've been trying to finish the tipi for Father," I stuttered. Then her face softened some.

"Well, where is it?" she asked.

"It's not finished yet . . ." I began to explain.

"We leave at dawn for winter camp. You must be finished by then, Coati. Your father gave you that task in front of the entire clan. He cannot allow you to back out. Besides, we will need it this winter."

"I will go and bring it back finished, Mother," I assured her. She patted my head and gave a strained smile. I smiled back and took off running toward Quatl's camp. I remembered to whistle for one of the camp dogs to follow me.

My mind was now racing as fast as my heart. I knew the tipi was nearly completed, but I was worried that it would not be good enough. What if it looked funny next to all of the tipis made by the older squaws? What if my father did not approve?

As I neared Quatl's camp, night had fallen and I could see his campfire glowing, down in the little draw where he was camped. The campfire's light danced on the side of the new tipi we had built. It looked just like the ones in our camp. It really was a fine tipi.

Why had Quatl helped me so much? Was it just because he was so lonely? I wondered if his days as an Apache slave gave him a softer heart than most braves. As I got closer, I could see that his stooped, old frame was busy shuffling around the tipi. What was he up to?

28

As I got nearer, I could see he was painting the out-side of the tipi. It is customary for both the inside and the outside of a tipi to be decorated with paint. The inside is usually painted by the squaw with decorative patterns. The outside is painted by the man of the fam-ily. He usually paints pictures that tell stories of his ac-complishments or of his family history.

I walked up to Quatl, who was busy painting a

scene. He said nothing, but he knew that I was there. I watched his gnarled old hands work the horsehair brush. He had great skill.

"I know that you must leave soon. The tribe is moving camp," he said after I had stood there for a while. "I am nearly finished."

He seemed to know exactly what our tribe was doing without ever being in camp. Eventually, he laid down the brush and picked up his old pipe and lit it. He placed his hand on my shoulder and led me to the entrance of the tipi.

"Let's start here," his old voice cracked. He pointed over the entrance to the picture of a wolf with a large tail. He held a torch near to illuminate it.

"This will tell everyone that this is your father's home." We began to walk around the tipi. The next picture was of a boy, many wolves, and an antelope.

"This is the story of your father's medicine. When he was a boy he crept in among a pack of wolves who were on the hunt. When the wolves began to chase the antelope, your father joined the chase. His hair trailed behind him just as the tail of a wolf when he ran. He became a brave that day."

A few steps more around the tipi and we came to the next painting. It was a picture of a battle. There were two groups of Indians and many horses.

"This was a great day for our tribe!" Quatl explained proudly. "We raided the Apache and won many horses. The horses made our tribe strong. There is your father. There is me. We were great warriors that day." His face beamed.

We moved to the next picture. By torchlight, I could see it was a picture of a very hard winter. Finally, we came to the last picture. Quatl stood before it for a long time. He put the pipe to his mouth once, and then again. The painting was of a great group of Indians. Our tribe.

"This is the story of our tribe," Quatl said slowly, pointing to the great mass of Indians he had drawn. Then he pointed to one baby drawn to the side by itself.

"This is new Comanches being born into our tribe. When the tribe is healthy and well-fed, many babies are born," he explained.

Then he pointed to another figure drawn by itself. This figure was painted with gray hair and a bent back. "This is an old Comanche. He is too old to hunt and fight. He has to leave the tribe to make room for new Comanches."

We stood quietly gazing at this last painting. Quatl had painted my father's story on the tipi, which was customary. But I saw that he had also told his own story too.

"I am very proud of this tipi. And I thank you for your help, Quatl," I told him as we stood admiring it. "Wherever our camp is, there your story will be told. Our people will remember you when they see this story. My father will be proud to have it on his tipi."

His only reply was to smile at me with his old toothless face.

Once we knew the paint was dry, Quatl and I took the tipi down as quickly as it had gone up. I no longer was worried about my father's reaction to the new tipi. I knew he would be pleased.

Quatl showed me how to roll the tipi covering around the poles and then to lash the poles to form a travois or sled, so that the tipi could be dragged. He then whistled for the dog. The dog had fallen asleep by the campfire, but he reluctantly got up and trotted over to where we stood. With a few leather thongs, Quatl harnessed the dog to the travois so the tipi could be carried back to our camp.

I thanked Quatl again and again, and I told him how much he had taught me. I think he was embarrassed. But as always, he seemed so kind. His only reply was to stroke my hair and pat my shoulder.

Finally, I started the walk back to our camp with the dog and the new tipi trailing behind me. Just as I was going to leave, Quatl's face perked up and he said, "Be careful not to burn this tipi down."

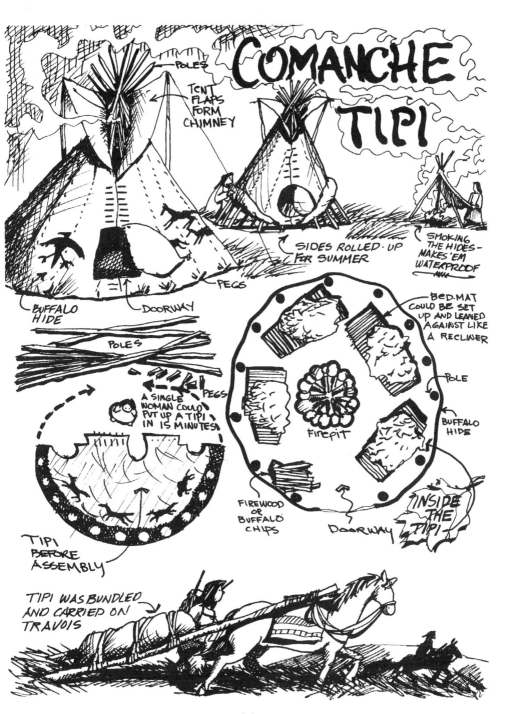

COMANCHE TIPI

POLES

TENT FLAPS FORM CHIMNEY

SIDES ROLLED·UP FOR SUMMER

SMOKING THE HIDES - MAKES 'EM WATERPROOF

BUFFALO HIDE

DOORWAY

PEGS

POLES

PEGS

BED·MAT COULD BE SET UP AND LEANED AGAINST LIKE A RECLINER

POLE

BUFFALO HIDE

A SINGLE WOMAN COULD PUT UP A TIPI IN 15 MINUTES!

FIREPIT

FIREWOOD OR BUFFALO CHIPS

DOORWAY

INSIDE THE TIPI

TIPI BEFORE ASSEMBLY

TIPI WAS BUNDLED AND CARRIED ON TRAVOIS

33

About the Comanche Tipi

It was probably in the 1600s that the Comanches changed their lifestyle. They went from being a Rocky Mountain tribe that hunted on foot to a plains tribe that chased the buffalo on horseback. When they made this change, they had to have a new kind of shelter that fit their life on the open plains. That is why the tipi was born.

The Comanches moved constantly to follow the buffalo herd, so they designed the tipi to be easy to set up and move. They had to have a shelter that could withstand the climate of the Great Plains, so they developed the tipi with sides that would roll up in the summer and be staked to the ground in the winter. Even the tipi's shape, the cone, was ideal for resisting the high winds of the plains.

Just like everything else the Comanches made, the tipi was made almost entirely of materials that came from the buffalo.

The Sod-House

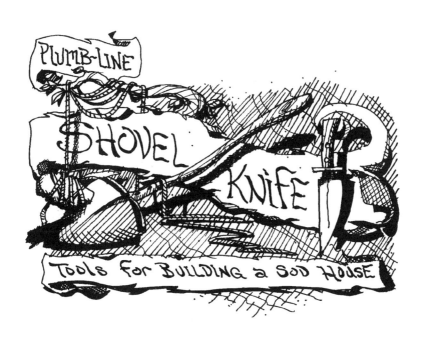

PLUMB-LINE

SHOVEL

KNIFE

Tools for Building a Sod House

Chapter 1

Daddy's Dying

He was a gruesome sight! The lantern showed my pappy's pale face pouring sweat onto the pillow under his old bald head. My momma, my little brother and me had been sitting in the covered wagon for a week now, just watching the fever kill my poor old pappy. Now, it seemed, the fever was almost done with him.

With all his strength, he lifted his bony hand from his side on the bed. It looked so strange as it trembled and hovered a few inches above his chest. I'd never watched someone die before. My pappy's trembling hand moved toward me now. His hand grabbed my shirt and pulled me close. My eyes met his. His mouth opened to speak.

"It's all on you now, Zeb . . . you and the Lord." He wheezed to catch his breath. "After the war, it didn't seem like those of us on the losing side had much to stick around for. So I brought you all out west to start over. This is as far as I got you. Winter's coming, so there's little time to waste."

He paused again. His lips trembled, but his eyes and his grip on me were still strong. His voice came again.

"Zeb . . . you see that shovel over there? After you're through burying me with it, don't you even lay it down. You just start right in to digging your momma a dugout house like we seen at that farm we passed in June. It won't be pretty, but it'll keep you from freezing to death when the northers blow across these plains."

His grip on my shirt loosened, and my pappy lay quiet again. My momma, who had cried herself dry days ago, leaned over and kissed his sweaty forehead.

"Lord Jesus," she prayed, "he's on his way home to see you." Those would be the last words spoken for several hours.

The four of us sat silently in the covered wagon until Pappy breathed his last. Then I did just as he told me. I retrieved the shovel from under the wagon seat and hopped to the ground.

Daylight was breaking on the flat, treeless landscape. Back home in the East, great pine trees keep you from seeing the sun till a good hour after sunrise. Not so here on these Texas plains. The sun barely winks at you over the horizon, and suddenly, everything is daylight with hardly a shadow anywhere.

I scanned the surroundings, looking for the right place for Pappy's remains to rest. Even though the whole countryside seemed flat as a pancake, I spied a long, low swell that rose slightly above the rest of the plains. I set out for it with my shovel in my hand and our hound dog at my heels.

38

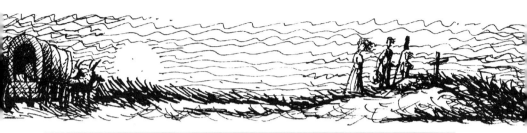

As I walked toward the site I had selected for Pappy's grave, I tried to decide whether or not I was scared of the prospect of being the "man of the family." I was nearly thirteen, so I was plenty old enough. Besides, when Pappy was off fighting Yankees with Stonewall, I was the man of the house then. I was pretty sure I was up to the task. Anyways, I was sure going to miss my old pappy.

After I had dug a proper grave for Pappy, I returned to the wagon. Momma and my brother Nathan were waiting for me. Our cow was still tied to the rear of the wagon, waiting to be milked.

It felt strange to swing onto the wagon seat. I now was sitting where Pappy had been for the last five months. Momma sat next to me and gave me a sad smile. I picked up the reins and murmured a "giddy-up" to the old mule. We took the short trip back to the grave that I had dug. It would have been easy to forget where it was on the grassy plains. But our hound was bounding toward it, so I just followed him.

After Pappy was placed in his grave, Nathan stuck a small cross of sticks at his head. Momma prayed the Shepherd's Psalm from memory. For a while, we stood around the little grave site, the first mark we had left on this strange, quiet land. When I felt like it was the right time, I led Momma a few yards from the grave site.

"Pappy said we should start right in on our homestead. All this land is for the taking, so I guess we can build anywhere we like," I said. Momma seemed to be collecting her thoughts back to this world. She gazed around the great stretch of grass and sky.

"Well, we need a place that is out of the north wind and close to the creek," she said. "You boys will be fetching a lot of water until we can dig a well."

Because of my momma's instruction, I had a picture in my head of Nathan and me lugging buckets of water to the house twice a day. I don't think until then I had ever thought much about how important it was to pick the right place for a house. The tough part was that, while there was plenty of land to choose from, there was little water near *any* of it. Momma and I decided to retrace our wagon's trail back to a little creek that we had crossed before Pappy's illness.

It was less than a mile to that spot on the trail where we had last seen water. It was a pretty little creek with a few cottonwoods scattered along it. Having our home nearby would provide us both water and a wood supply.

I told Momma that we would drive the wagon along this creek until we found a place deep enough to dip a bucket in. Once we did, we figured it wouldn't be too wise to build our new home right on the bank of the creek in case it ever flooded. We'd seen this happen on the plains before. One minute a little creek like this pokes along quietly; next minute it's a raging bull of a river. All because there's a thunder squall upstream somewhere. So we pulled the wagon about fifty man-size paces away from the creek.

Next, we had to check the wind. All three of us hopped down from the wagon. I picked up a piece of grass and tossed it up in the air. Since it was already October and feeling a little like November, I knew that even the breeze would be from the north. The little piece of grass took flight to the south. The three of us strolled over to a little hill that shrugged its shoulders just ever so slightly above the rest of the sweeping plains. We decided we could build our home on the hill's south side and get a little protection from the winter winds.

The three of us stood there in the spot we'd chosen and surveyed the surroundings. Water and wood nearby. A gentle slope for good drainage. A little elevation to the north for wind protection. Plenty of grass for our stock. Nice stretches of flatland for farming and, hopefully, a little wild game to put on the table.

This seemed like it would be our new home, so we paused to give thanks.

Chapter 2

Diggin' Into A Surprise

Now that we picked us a good location, it was time to start building. Momma said we'd live out of the wagon until the dugout was finished, so she began setting up the kitchen right there on the prairie. I was glad to see her send Nathan off to fetch water and firewood, but I knew it wouldn't last long. He'd be back pestering me to help before I knew it, so I had to get to work quickly. It was time to play like I was one of those architects back East.

With shovel in hand, I paced off a rectangle in the grass about ten feet wide and twenty feet long. This would be the house we'd live in. To save some work, I decided to actually make the back wall of the house the face of the hill. I remembered that Pappy always said, "Take care of the animals first, the humans can wait." So I walked off a rectangle for a stable just a few yards downwind from our house.

I felt pretty confident now as I looked at the stakes I had set at each of the four corners of the house and the stable. The chill in the breeze reminded me that I hadn't much time. We would be sleeping out in the open until the job was done.

Nathan was now at my side, eager to help in this manly project. I explained to him that the stakes in the ground marked the corners of our house and stable. Cutting out the sod or grass in between the stakes was our first step. The farmer that Pappy had talked to last summer explained that it was like "cutting up sheet cake." You just divide the cake up in little squares with your shovel and lift them out. Each piece of sod would be used like a building block to build the walls.

So as I cut up the sod in squares about two feet by two feet, Nathan pulled them up and stacked them out of the way. I've never seen a kid enjoy getting his hands so dirty. Even our hound dog stood by smelling the fresh earth as each piece of sod came up.

After we pulled all the sods up, the square hole in the ground was only about eighteen inches deep. The farmer whose house we'd seen had said that if you dig down deeper you will stay warmer in the winter. So, I

started digging out the extra dirt. This was really tough work, so I let Nathan help all he wanted. When Momma called us to eat, I realized we'd been working for hours.

Eating was taken care of in short order. Partly because there was still much to do and partly because every stop in the work gave us time to think of Pappy's loss.

There was more digging to do just to get the hole deep enough. Since the hillside would be our back wall, we had to dig into it so that it would be nice and straight, up and down. As I was digging into the hillside, I sunk the shovel into a soft area in the dirt when all of a sudden, the ground seemed to explode. Dirt was flying, the hound was bellowing, and a hissing noise filled the air. I jumped back several feet, holding the shovel like a rifle. There, standing in the middle of what would be our living room, was a very angry badger!

It seems we had dug into his living quarters, and he was not at all happy about it. We knew this because he was baring his teeth, just daring us to take him on. I had often heard how these prairie badgers would take on animals twice their size and win. About that time, Momma joined us with the old muzzle-loader rifle.

As soon as Momma entered the scene of the standoff with the rifle, Nathan piped up, "Can I shoot 'im? Can I shoot 'im?"

The three of us looked at the fierce snarling creature. He was not even as big as our dog, but, by reputation, we knew he was not to be taken lightly. Still, none of us was hungry enough to eat badger. And we hoped not to be anytime soon. And it didn't seem right to shoot the old fellow just to replace his burrow with ours.

So instead, I quickly walked over to Momma's cooking fire and fished out a flaming limb. Then I walked toward the hissing badger, holding the torch in front of me. The badger slowly backed into the hole we had tore in his den until he disappeared.

"Well, now how are we going to get rid of him?" Nathan complained. "Who's going to move out, him or us?"

Since I knew that the badger was a better builder than we were, I decided that he would be the one to move. So I pitched the torch into his hole and covered it with a gunny sack.

"Come on!" I said, and ran around the hill to the other side. The three of us reached the north side of the knoll in time to see smoke billowing out of the badger's front door. A few seconds later, out stormed the badger.

I figured a badger would even fight fire, but he couldn't fight smoke. We watched as he waddled off to homestead a new hillside and leave us his old one.

Chapter 3

Sod Stackin'

By the end of that first day we felt like we had done well. Without old Pappy to help us, we'd found a good site for our new farm. We'd done most of our digging, and we'd even done battle with a badger. Nathan and I had dug by firelight late into that frosty evening. Momma had dug, too, and brought us biscuits and bacon. She didn't even say much about us eating with dirt-crusted fingers.

When we finally quit to sleep in the wagon, we were all too tired to even speak. But we all knew without speaking how right Pappy had been about getting this place built as soon as possible. Snow was coming. You could smell it. We slept well, relying on the hound and the mules to keep night watch.

Next day came early and cold. Sore muscles were not in short supply. Momma stoked the cooking fire, Nathan tended the livestock, and I went straight to work on the dugout.

That day would be a day of stacking up the walls. Since we dug the floor of the house down to three feet below the ground, we would only have to build the walls four or five feet high. That would be plenty to get high enough for a full grown man to stand up inside. I used myself as a measuring stick against the dugout hillside, and eyeballed where I thought the roof would be.

Our walls would be built by stacking the sods on top of each other. Each sod really was like a square slice of cake. The grass on top of each sod chunk was like the frosting, and the dirt attached to it was like the fluffy cake part. The fine hairy roots of the grass held the dirt together. The hard part was keeping the walls going straight up and down. I'd seen some masons in Atlanta using a plumb line to be sure their brick walls stayed straight. So I decided to do the same. I don't know if this was the frontier way or not, but there was no one around to ask. I used some string and a rock to make my plumb line. I knew that the gravity on the rock would always keep the string straight up and down. I would use this to check my walls.

About the time I figured all this out, Nathan showed up with some biscuits and bacon Momma had made for us. We gave thanks and prayed for the Lord's help on our efforts. We ate breakfast while I explained to Nathan how we were going to build the walls. On an easier day, Nathan would have thought of something to argue about. But the cold morning kept reminding us how important it was to get Momma an indoor kitchen. So we started right into stacking sods.

It was pretty quick work. The walls were going to be

two feet thick since that's how wide we cut the sods. We hoped that was going to be all right. Like I said, there was no one around to ask.

When it came time to make the windows, we had to stop and scratch our heads for a while. Of course, we had no glass or window frames. The window would just be a hole in the wall. I had to figure out how to support the dirt above the window opening. I tried to picture the one dugout we had seen before. It seemed like that old farmer had used boards to bridge over the windows. On top of those boards, he stacked the sods.

I sent Nathan to take an empty barrel apart and bring me five staves — one stave for each window and one for the door. This seemed to work just fine. Only problem was that the windows and door could only be as wide as the wooden stave. I decided to have one window on each of the short sides of our house, and I'd put two windows and the door on the long side that faced the south. I hoped this arrangement would give us good air flow in the hot, dry summers. I didn't put any windows in the stable, just one big doorway. That would be safer for the livestock.

Well, we only needed a foot or two of sods above the windows and we were ready to talk about the roof. I figured the roof could be supported by small trees that we would cut down from the creek, but Momma was quick to point out that we needed those trees to grow and make kindling for our fire every year. Kindling, or "squaw wood," is all the small branches that die and drop off of a tree every year. Instead of chopping down the whole tree, Nathan and I just chopped off limbs

large enough to support the roof. If we spaced these roof support beams pretty close together, they didn't have to be much thicker than my wrist.

Most of the rest of the day was spent cutting and hauling limbs from the creek to the house and stable. We used the mule team for that. We would tie the long limbs into a sort of bundle. Then we let the mules drag the bundle kind of like an Indian travois. Nathan was trying to ride the load of limbs as the mules drug them back to the house, but he kept getting his fingers pinched in between the logs. Served him right!

Chapter 4

There's a Reason for That Fence

About the time we had all the wood that we thought we would need, Momma came and told us to call it quits for the day. She insisted we sit down and eat a proper supper and get some rest.

"Well, it's going to be our last night under the stars!" I boasted. "Tomorrow night we'll be sitting down to eat in our new soddie and sleeping under a roof!"

Momma smiled. She wouldn't have complained if we weren't finished for another week. You could always count on Momma to be steady.

A proper supper it was too. At least as proper as you could have, sitting around a campfire on barrels. Nathan didn't have any better manners than our old hound, so it couldn't be too proper, no matter where we were sitting. But the food was especially good and was quickly followed by some shut-eye.

Yesterday started off colder than the day before,

and today was even colder than that. But we felt encouraged because today would be the day for putting on the roof on both the house and the stable. So we fell to our work with whistles and hums. The arm-thick limbs were laid on top of the walls about twelve inches apart. We cut them to the right length with the axe. (I don't hardly know how one would get along without an axe. It's got to be the handiest tool a man ever had. Even the Indians, who never seemed to have bothered with the wheel, have always had some sort of axe.) We left these roof beams to overhang the walls some, so that the roof would provide some shade.

After the beams were in place, we cut more sod for the roof. This time Momma told us where the corn and vegetables would be planted, so that's where we cut the sod. We'd have to clear the thick prairie grass from there anyway.

The first layer of sod we laid with the grassy side down. I hoped this would keep the dirt from falling on us as it dried out. The next layer of sod we laid on a thin layer of loose dirt. This was my own idea. I was hoping the sod on the roof would continue to grow grass in the spring. I figured the roof would last longer if the grass was alive.

While we were laying the roof, Momma was cutting up old rugs and clothes for curtains to hang in the windows. These weren't for looks, but to keep out cold air.

I sent Nathan down to stomp on the floor in our house. The floor of our soddie would just be bare dirt, but at least it would be flat. You've never seen a kid better suited to a job than Nathan was to stomping. I finally had to tell him to quit after about an hour.

Packing The Floor

There was lots of little things to take care of, but our house was nearly habitable. One big chore was left — putting in the stove. Our old cast-iron stove that we brought with us from back East would be the center of the house. It was used for heating the home and cooking the meals. Back East, wood would have been burned in the stove. But here on the prairie, bundles of grass and buffalo chips would be the fire's fuel, most of the time.

53

Just getting the heavy iron stove out of the wagon was a job. We backed the wagon up to the house's door. I was now wishing I had put the stove in before we built the walls. Oh, well. Now we'd have to unload it at the front door and carry it a few feet to its final resting place.

To get it out of the wagon, I hooked up a sort of

windlass so I could lower it using ropes instead of my back. If there'd been another man around, we could have lifted it without any such contrivance. But I was afraid, with just the three of us, someone could get hurt moving such a heavy object. And if someone did get hurt, it was a long way to a doctor.

Well, with much sweat and grunting, we bullied that old black stove into place. Once there, we then cut a hole in the roof for the flue pipe. This let the smoke out. I had to prop up the pipe above the roof. I wanted it to stick up pretty high, so the wind would make it draw the smoke real good. If it didn't work, the smoke would sting our eyes and make us cough, down inside the house.

My, my, my, were we proud of ourselves! It was near the end of the third day and we had ourselves a house and a stable. Even though the house was mostly dirt and grass, it looked mighty comfortable to us. After all, we'd been sleeping in the open for several months now. Momma could now cook breakfast in the warm kitchen rather than on an open fire, and we'd be sleeping with a roof over our heads. We were happy! Since it was getting dark, we all rushed to take care of odds and ends before supper. Momma said supper would be special.

I told Nathan to see to the stock. We'd been letting the mules and the cow graze all around the open prairie while we were working, but now it was time to introduce them to their new stable.

I moved the rest of our belongings from the wagon to the soddie. There was a trunk full of clothes and keepsakes, kerosene lamps, and a few sticks of furniture. I brought in the old blankets and I stuffed the ticks with new prairie grass so they'd be soft and good-smelling. (Ticks are like big sacks that are stuffed with grass or straw to sleep on.)

Well, supper was ready and it was indeed special. Before we fell to eating it, though, we gave thanks. I prayed, "Oh Lord, thank you that you always give your creatures what they need to live on. Even on the desolate prairie, You show us Your abundance of provisions that You've stockpiled, just waiting to be used. By Your hand, we are warm and content tonight. Amen."

We all ate till we felt stuffed like those ticks I filled with fresh grass. By the warmth of the stove, we sat and Momma picked a few tunes on the lap-harp. We could hear the wind blowing outside, but we felt none of it.

Exhausted and full, we lay down to sleep. In my head, I was picturing our soddie and the one we'd seen last summer. I was comparing details, trying to see if I forgot anything. There was one feature of that old farmer's soddie that I couldn't figure out. He'd built a fence across the back of his house. For the life of me, I couldn't figure out why. Oh well, I'd worry about that tomorrow. Speaking of tomorrow, "Nathan?" I whispered.

"Yeah?" he muttered, half asleep.

"Did you tie up the cow in the stable?" I asked.

"Nope. She didn't like the stable, so I left her outside," he mumbled.

"You *what?*" That was the last thing I remembered. Out of nowhere, the entire roof of the soddie came crashing down around our heads. Dust and grass and wood beams were all a flurry. And mixed in with our

screams and shouts was the terrified bellowing of our cow. She had grazed her way onto the roof of our soddie and fallen in on top of us!

I pushed off a blanket of sod and tree limbs and jumped to my feet. What had a minute ago been the warm, earthy smell of our dugout was now a choking, swirling cloud of dust and cold air. The culprit, our milking cow, was still bellowing and struggling to free herself from the wreckage of our roof. I gave her hindquarter an angry slap and she freed herself and pranced through the doorway.

Nathan's filthy face poked through a pile of sod. His white eyes blinked at the winter sky now open to us.

"Are you all right?" I asked in a disgusted tone.

"Uh-huh," he coughed. He seemed confused and dazed.

"Momma!" I shouted.

We could hear a groan from under a pile of roof beams and logs. Nathan and I worked to unpile the mess until we found Momma. Her pretty face and hair were covered with dust. She only groaned and held her arm in pain. We both leaned over and found a large lump in her upper left arm.

"Is . . . it . . . broke?" Nathan stammered.

"Yeah. Bad," I told him. "We got to find a doctor to set it. Go tie up that blasted cow like I told you the first time. Then hitch up the mules. Hurry!"

I spent the next few minutes trying to clean up Momma's face and make her comfortable. I could hear the jangling of bridles and reins in the background, so I knew Nathan was bringing the wagon to the door.

Momma groaned again as we lifted her onto some blankets in the back of the wagon. We covered her up. I knew with a break this painful, she could go into shock.

"Nathan!" I barked as I jumped to the seat of the wagon. "You stay here and watch the cow. I'll be back in a day or two." He didn't say a word. He handed me a lit lantern, trying everything he could to be helpful. He knew we had a real mess on our hands. And he knew I was real mad. I hated to leave Nathan alone. But the cow was too slow to take with us and too valuable to leave behind.

A sharp "giddy-up" and the mules pulled our wagon out onto the sea of grass. All I knew to do was head back down the trail that brought us here. I had no idea where to find another human being, much less a doctor.

"You doing all right, Momma?" I shouted to the back of the wagon.

"I'm okay," she stated calmly. She always seemed calm at times like this. "Zeb, don't be angry with Nathan. He's just a child."

"I know," I replied. And I knew she was right. My anger with Nathan was now being replaced by anger with myself. Just minutes ago, I was basking in my pride that I had put a roof over my family's head. Now I just felt dumb. I should have checked on the cow myself. Leastways, now I knew what that fence at the farmer's soddie was for. It was for keeping the blasted cows off the roof.

Several hours had passed since sundown and it was getting mighty cold. Icy prairie winds jabbed at every opening in my clothes. I pulled an extra blanket around my shoulders and kept scanning the dark plains for a light or some sign of human habitation. I could have been in the middle of the ocean, for all I could see was a big, starry sky and roll after roll of waving grass.

I was praying hard by now. I knew I had to get Momma to a doctor. There's no way I could set a broken bone like that. All I knew to do was keep heading east till I came to something.

After I topped a low swell, I finally saw a light and headed the mules straight for it at a good pace. It could have been a campfire or a light in a window. I couldn't tell yet.

It's amazing how far you can see on the plains. I went nearly a mile before I was close enough to see it was a campfire I was heading for. A few more minutes, and I pulled into a campsite ringed by two covered wagons and a bunch of livestock tethered to a rope. I pulled the team along a gap between their two wagons.

A young man with a rifle cradled in his left arm was standing near the fire, watching my every move. Before he could speak, I called to him in as friendly a voice as I could muster, "Any doctors in this camp?"

All of a sudden, what had been a quiet camp now bristled with sleepy faces of all ages. From the back of wagons and from under blankets, heads poked out to see what the commotion was. There must have been twenty or thirty sets of eyes watching me. I figured this must be at least two families on their way out west.

"What's the problem?" said the man with the rifle. I could tell he was not quite comfortable with me yet.

"It's my mother. She's got a broke arm," I returned. This seemed to break the ice, because the whole camp erupted with "oh my's " and *"mmm-mmm's."* I just let them chatter for a minute. Finally, an older fellow spoke up.

"We passed a stagecoach relay station today. There was a doctor putting up there for the night. If you ride towards the Canadian River from here, you might catch him before the stage leaves at dawn," he explained.

I hung on every word. As soon as he was through, I said a quick thanks and headed in the direction that he had pointed.

Chapter 5

Soddie, Sweet Soddie

Well, I didn't get to the stagecoach station before the doctor left. But I did leave Momma and the wagon at the station with the old couple there while I chased down the stage on a borrowed horse. I must've looked like I meant business because I didn't have too much trouble convincing them to turn the stagecoach around.

When they returned, Momma got her arm set so it would heal real good, and the folks at the station even fed us a hot meal. I couldn't pay the doctor anything but my appreciation. He didn't seem to mind.

We were back on the trail to our soddie (or what was left of it) by noon. I hoped we'd be home before midnight. Momma was resting much more comfortable now. Every jolt of the wagon wasn't making her cringe now that her arm was set between two planks. It was still going to be a long ride home.

In fact, on the way home, that blue norther we'd

been fearing for the last week finally caught up with us. The wind gusted, and dark clouds filled the sky, and then the snow started. Going home to a soddie with no roof, in a snow storm, was going to be no treat.

My spirits weren't too high. I don't think I said much all the way home.

Snow covered everything with a nice smooth blanket by the time we reached the creek that ran near our house. It was well past dark and the snow had a blue-gray color under the night sky. In my head, I was figuring on how to fix our roof. I was trying to decide if I was too tired to start right in on it, or if I should wait till dawn.

As I pulled around the little hill that hid our soddie from the north, I couldn't believe my eyes. It wasn't the wrecked structure filling up with snow that I expected. No, this soddie had a roof and smoke curling out of the flue pipe. The windows glowed with lamplight and warmth.

I stopped the wagon and looked all around me. Did I get lost? Was this someone else's farm? No, this must be the place, I thought. Could Nathan have fixed all this on his own? In two days? The only way to find out was to go inside. Momma was beginning to wake up.

"Wait here, Momma," I said softly as I hopped down from the wagon. The smell of cooking greeted my nose as I neared the door. Now I *knew* Nathan hadn't done all of this. I pulled aside the blanket that served as a front door and peeked in. I was sure I was in the wrong place. This soddie was packed with people, and they were all staring back at the surprised look on my face.

"Oh, excuse me," I stammered and began to back out of the doorway.

"Hey, Zeb!" came Nathan's familiar voice. "Is Momma all right?"

I stopped and peered around the room until I located Nathan's face in the crowd. He was a little hard to recognize because he had strawberry jam from one ear to another. Now I was really confused. But while I was standing there with my mouth open, an older man stepped forward to greet me.

"I hope you don't mind, but after we saw you the other night, we happened upon your place here." I now recognized this fellow from the campsite that I had stopped at looking for a doctor.

He went on to explain how they found Nathan struggling to fix the roof all by himself, and figured he'd needed some help. Well, with all the helping hands in their party, it didn't take no time to fix the roof. They even took care of a few other chores, like bundling grass for the stove. He said that the weather had turned mean and he was hoping I wouldn't mind if they stayed there till the weather broke.

As he was explaining all this, someone was shoving a plate full of biscuits into my hand. I was so delighted to see the roof fixed, what could I say? I almost forgot to get Momma out of the wagon.

It was a regular celebration. I'm still not sure how we got all those folks into our little soddie. That was the biggest family I've ever seen.

"We're going to be your new neighbors," a green-eyed girl about my age chirped.

I smiled. Things was going to be all right — as soon as I got that fence built, that is.

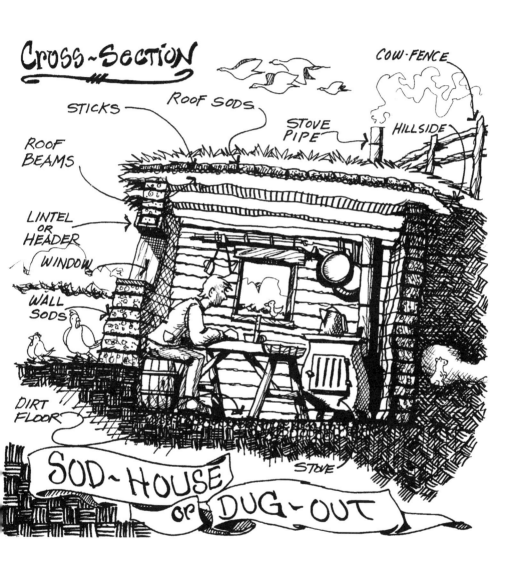

CROSS-SECTION

COW-FENCE

STICKS

ROOF SODS

STOVE PIPE

HILLSIDE

ROOF BEAMS

LINTEL OR HEADER

WINDOW

WALL SODS

DIRT FLOOR

STOVE

SOD-HOUSE or DUG-OUT

65

About the Settler's Dugout of the 1800s

A "soddie" or dugout was the perfect dwelling for the plains settler of the 1800s. This type of house made use of two building materials that were in great abundance: dirt and grass.

The pioneer only needed a few tools to build a soddie. With his shovel, he would cut eighteen-inch-wide strips of grass and dirt out of the grassy plains. He would then stack these one on top of another to make the walls. To make the roof, wood poles or planks were laid on top of the walls, bridging from side to side. These poles were then covered with a couple of layers of sod. The only difference between the soddie and the dugout is that a dugout could be built half underground or into a hillside.

These dirt homes did leak when it rained and were dusty in the summer, but they were inexpensive and quickly built. Furthermore, they stayed relatively cool in the summer and warm in the winter. As with all useful architecture, these structures were a good combination of available technology and local materials.

From Dog-Trot
to Mansion

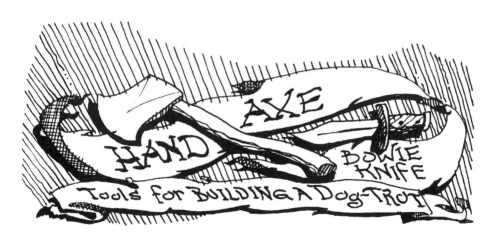

Tools for BUILDING A Dog-TROT

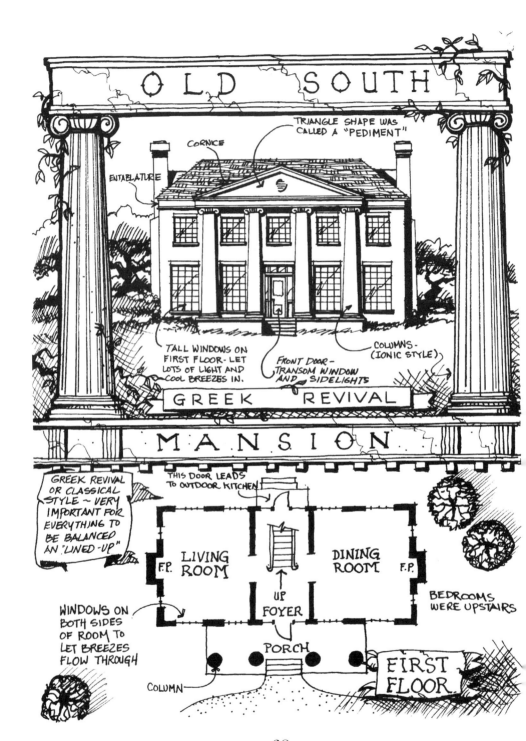

OLD SOUTH

TRIANGLE SHAPE WAS CALLED A "PEDIMENT"

CORNICE

ENTABLATURE

TALL WINDOWS ON FIRST FLOOR- LET LOTS OF LIGHT AND COOL BREEZES IN.

FRONT DOOR - TRANSOM WINDOW AND SIDELIGHTS

COLUMNS - (IONIC STYLE)

GREEK REVIVAL

MANSION

GREEK REVIVAL OR CLASSICAL STYLE ~ VERY IMPORTANT FOR EVERYTHING TO BE BALANCED AN "LINED-UP"

THIS DOOR LEADS TO OUTDOOR KITCHEN

LIVING ROOM

F.P.

DINING ROOM

F.P.

BEDROOMS WERE UPSTAIRS

UP FOYER

WINDOWS ON BOTH SIDES OF ROOM TO LET BREEZES FLOW THROUGH

PORCH

COLUMN

FIRST FLOOR

Chapter 1

Frontier Architect

The sawing of saws and pounding of hammers makes a construction site a mighty noisy place. But to me that noise is like music. It seems I've always been at construction sites. I kinda grew up there. You see, my father is Angus McBride, Master Builder and Architect, and I am his apprentice. I was listening to all the noises as we inspected the construction of a new house, a big house for James Kern. Mr. Kern owns the largest plantation in this part of Texas these days, in the 1850s.

Well, as I was saying, we were strolling about the construction site when the "music" was broken by loud, angry German voices. My ears didn't understand a word of it, but my eyes could see that two barrel-chested German carpenters were squared-off for a fist fight. Clouds of dust were being raised by their shuffling feet as they moved about trying to get in a good punch.

In a second, my father sprang from my side into the

middle of the two. I had to laugh at the scene. My father is not too big. And in his neat waistcoat and riding boots, he looked like a well-dressed cricket trying to separate a couple of growling badgers.

With a few words from my father, the two carpenters went back to pounding nails rather than each other. I rejoined my father and we continued to stroll around the construction site.

"Blasted Germans!" my father snorted to me in a low voice laced with his Scottish accent. "They're even more stubborn than our ancestors, Tommy-boy." He smiled and winked at me as he said it.

"What on earth were they fighting about?" I asked.

Carving an Ionic Column

"If you can believe this, they were fighting over who was the best carpenter. You see, both of them were making one of the huge columns for the front of the house. They were arguing about which way to carve the flutings — should they be rounded or squared at the end?"

"Well, what did you say?" I asked.

"I told them to flip a coin or something. But all the columns had better match, I told them. I don't want half of them rounded and half of them squared!"

We both chuckled a little. "What they are really fighting about is that they are frustrated," my father continued. "Here they are in a new land, with no money, no land, and working like dogs in this Texas heat." He mopped his thin red face with his kerchief.

"You could have bought some slaves for this job," I reminded him. "Mr. Kern would have gladly loaned you some of his slaves to work on his house."

"I know . . . I know . . ." Angus repeated with a sigh. "I've just got no stomach for slaves. I prefer to buy a man's sweat and labor. I do not care to own his life."

Yes, it's true. Even though my father's job is building beautiful plantation houses for slave owners like Mr. Kern, he secretly hates the idea of slavery. Why, he would rather ride all the way to Indianola and hire German immigrants at good wages than use slaves on his construction jobs. When Mr. Kern asked why he was willing to spend more money to hire those carpenters, he said it was because they were better trained. But in truth, my father would have sawed each board himself before he would use a slave on one of his jobs.

Now, you may be asking yourself how someone who

71

detests slavery can get along in a slave state like Texas in the 1850s. But really, only a few people like the plantation owners hold slaves. Most folks in Texas are small farmers, working hard themselves on their own little family farms.

Well, here I go again. I'm supposed to be telling a story about building a big, beautiful plantation home, but instead I'm talking about people and all of their problems, rather than boards, and nails, and beams. But, you know, my father Angus says that's not surprising. He says buildings, especially houses, are like storybooks of who people are and what their dreams are.

So as I tell you this story of the building of a house for Mr. Kern, I'll warn you that you'll learn a bit about people too.

Chapter 2

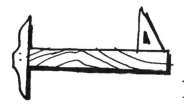 # A Mansion for the Kerns

It was a nice autumn day. The summer's heat had given away grudgingly to the fall winds. I was sitting on a hill admiring the house my father had, just that week, finished building.

On that breezy hilltop, the wind kept tugging at the pages of my sketchbook while I was trying to draw. Anyway, I was used to drawing outdoors and I was pretty satisfied with the way this sketch was shaping up.

I was really bearing down on some of the details of my artwork when a thick Scottish voice boomed from behind me. I nearly jumped out of my boots! But it was only my father, Angus McBride. He is the best architect in this part of Texas. It is also true that he is just about the *only* architect out here.

Still, I think quite highly of the houses he designs and builds, and I like being his apprentice. That's why I was sitting on that hilltop with a sketchbook. Part of my

training as an architect's apprentice is learning to draw the houses and buildings we build. My father said it would train my eye to see details. He has me carry that sketchbook every place but the outhouse.

As I got better at it, I actually came to like the drawing and sketching. I especially like drawing the big homes of wealthy plantation owners. Those big houses have such finely detailed columns and windows. Painted in bright whitewash, they look like some kind of dream out there in the Texas wilderness. In fact, that is what I was drawing that day, the grand new home of Master James Kern.

My father slid to a seat in the grass next to me. He inspected my work for a second, then went back to reading the mail he picked up from the stagecoach that day.

"Interesting letter from me uncle in Chicago," he said as he was reading. "It seems that he has opened an elegant new hotel." My father read some more and then chuckled. "He wants his hotels to have southern charm and hospitality, but he can find no workers that possess such rare qualities." My uncle's predicament seemed to really tickle my father's sense of humor. Scots have a peculiar idea of what's funny.

My father continued in a snickering voice, "Hoot, mon! . . . he'd have as much luck catching a whale in the Mississippi as find a genteel southerner in Chicago. Even if a poor lad arrived there, with any manners at all, they would be quickly stolen!"

After my father quit chuckling, he pulled some newspaper and magazine clippings from the envelope that had held his uncle's letter. The magazine clippings were pictures of houses and banks and hotels back East. Pictures are very important to a frontier architect like my father because that is how he keeps up with the latest building styles in the big eastern cities. And believe me, plantation owners are very concerned with having their houses look just as stylish as the ones in Charleston and Richmond.

"Ah . . . here's a pretty one, Tommy-boy," my father exclaimed. (Yes, he really does call me Tommy-boy.) He had found a clipping of a house built in the same style as the one that I was sketching.

"You see the tall columns along the front, supporting the pediment creating a great entrance porch. Oh . . . and here . . . the tall windows for the first story and the slightly shorter ones on the second floor. And it's all arranged in such an orderly fashion. It's a fine example of that Greek Revival style that all these planters are wanting."

My father's enthusiasm for the newspaper picture was a tad too much, but he got that way every time we got clippings in the mail. Like most professionals on the frontier in the 1850s, my father has had little in the way of formal education. Most of his architectural training has been self-taught from magazine clippings and books he can borrow. My father always says, "On the frontier, a man can be almost anything he is bold enough to claim to be . . . *If* he is disciplined enough to teach himself." He called this "frontier resourcefulness."

Now, even though I was the one drawing this thing, I wasn't sure I understood why the house we'd just built for Master Kern was called a "Greek Revival" house. To me, the phrase "Greek Revival" reminds me of the snake oil the traveling medicine shows sell. Of course, my father was more than eager to explain to me what "Greek Revival" meant.

"Well, Tommy-boy, it's like this . . . A person could fuss over this detail or that detail, but in my mind, it really comes down to the front porches of the houses. They look like an ancient Greek Temple. . . like the Acropolis."

"What on earth is a Greek temple doing on the Texas frontier?" I asked.

My father really got a laugh from that question, but as always, he had an answer.

"Now, Tommy-boy, your question has struck on one of the truly odd things about architecture. You see, designing and building a house for someone is not just about bricks, and beams, and such, but it's also about folks' dreams of who they are, and who they want to be.

"These cotton planters with their huge plantations and all their slaves, they see themselves as being like knights from the Middle Ages with their estates being worked by the peasants. Or like the ancient Greek nobles who had vast family estates and an army of slaves to work it."

I know I looked rather puzzled at this notion, so my father added, "These southern gentlemen are a romantic lot. They have a real love for the past. Look at their concern with chivalry, and manners, and such. This evening at Mr. Kern's housewarming party, take a peek at his bookshelf and tell me what you see."

"A party at Mr. Kern's house!" I exclaimed. I had nearly forgotten.

"Hold your seat, lad," my father chuckled. "You finish your drawing and we'll head down to the house when we see the other guests arrive."

As I continued to draw, my eye roved over the vast estate to find features to include in my drawing. I was satisfied with the house, so I drew in the tall pines that lined the road which led to the house. Then I sketched in the lush green lawn where some fine black horses were grazing. My father had commented that one of those horses would probably be our payment for designing and building Mr. Kern's house. This wouldn't be unusual because cash money is scarce, even among the wealthy plantation owners. My father has been paid by other clients in livestock, land, and even furniture.

After I sketched in the horses in the pasture, I gazed out over the rolling cotton fields. It was late in the day now, so Master Kern's army of African slaves was beginning to leave their work in the fields. Each tired-looking slave shouldered a bag filled with the white cotton bolls they had picked from the little plants.

The slaves have always had a strange effect on my father. As comfortable and confident my father is in socializing with the upper crust of our society, I can tell that slavery is something he really feels awkward about.

Chapter 3

The Party

Well, it wasn't long after the slaves had left the fields that guests began to arrive to see Master Kern's new house. I wondered if ol' Angus was ready for all of the attention each guest was going to lavish over his work. Each stair rail, each door frame, each room that my father had designed would be examined and politely praised by each guest. And hopefully, they would mean it. We would know for sure if the guests were truly impressed when, in a few weeks, one of them hired us to design and build a new house.

"Well, Tommy-boy, it looks like the party is about to start. Shall we make our entrance?" my father suggested.

I closed my sketchbook and slipped it into my coat pocket. We both mounted our horses and trotted down the hillside. In a moment we had joined the procession of guests on the road to the Kerns' grand front porch.

Horse-drawn carriages carried well-dressed couples. Single men were also sprinkled into the line on horseback. They were gallant fellows and politely tipped their hat to every female they encountered. The procession moved along slowly because the line ended at the Kerns' doorstep, where a trio of smartly dressed servants would help each guest from their carriage while ol' Jamesie Kern himself would greet them warmly.

It was great fun to be riding up to the house that we had designed and built. I was truly proud of our work. Against the dusky gray background of trees at sunset, the great white columns of the house made this feel like a very special place.

My father reminded me that this *is* an important place. Being the largest plantation in our part of Texas, Mr. Kern's home serves as a meeting place of sorts, a kind of unofficial capitol for our county. Everyone who could put on a shirt and two matching shoes had come to the party. It was a sort of town meeting. One of Mr. Kern's most admirable qualities is his hospitality, and he has the ability to make each guest feel welcome.

As our place in the procession finally reached the porch, James Kern was still there to greet us.

"Mighty fine-looking house, wouldn't you say, Angus?" Mr. Kern beamed.

"I'd be a poor guest if I didn't agree with you," joked my father. Mr. Kern surveyed the new house and stated boldly, "When a man can build a little piece of cultural refinement like this house, it makes you feel like we might whip this ol' wilderness after all."

Mr. Kern was right about the house being a bit of

cultural refinement, at least by frontier standards. A house like this is a far cry from the cabins, shacks, and dog-trots that many folks live in.

Inside the front door, a great entry hall opened up to us. Each room could be found from this hallway. Mrs. Kern scurried about the house, politely answering questions and commenting on various small-talk. Many of the men had broken into small groups, talking politics and Comanche raids. I would have been pretty relaxed if my father hadn't been elbowing me in the ribs every time a certain girl my age was spotted. So I tried to change the subject, every time he started talking about how nice all the women folk looked.

As we stepped through the doorway, our world seemed to transform. I saw all the familiar hard, hot faces of the frontier people. But instead of the hard-working, sweaty faces they usually wore, here they had on festive faces that joked and told stories. And everyone was on their best behavior. Even ol' Ben Johnson, one of the Texas Rangers, looked different. My father said it was the absence of chewing tobacco dripping from his chin.

"Isn't it strange how a new building can make folks act? Can buildings and houses and such really change people?" I asked my father as we surveyed the entry hall and its grand stairway to the second floor.

"Naw . . . only the Good Lord can truly change folks. But a house or building, like a courthouse, can symbolize something special to people."

That was the last question I asked my father for several hours because everyone at that party took turns congratulating him on what a grand house he had designed. Then they would suggest some improvement they had conjured up. I wondered if folks ever went up to doctors with such advice.

While my father was enjoying his moment of triumph, I enjoyed all the apple pie and cider I could stand. For a while, that "certain girl" and I took turns trying to look at each other. But mostly, I marveled as folks, who I knew usually used their sleeve as a napkin, tried to figure out what to do with all of the different kinds of forks and cups and saucers they were handed.

In frilly dresses and fancied hair, the women at this gathering all looked their best from head to toe. A lot of the men were a different story. Their top halves and bottom halves didn't seem to match. Up top, they'd be in a clean, white shirt with a vest and a tie. But their lower halves would still be tattered trousers and dusty boots.

All in all, the most impressive fellow at this gathering was Jethro, the Kerns' house servant. I admired his poised expression, his solemn black face and neat gray hair. I think he could have made a barn feel elegant with his humble dignity and perfect manners. House servants like Jethro were far different from the poor field hands who picked cotton all day. His job was to make the Kerns' guests feel welcome and important. Jethro took such pride in his craft, you would've thought he owned the place. He moved smoothly and swiftly through the house, making sure everyone was enjoying themselves.

Late in the evening, I took my father's suggestion and found my way to Mr. Kern's study. On display in this stately room was a wide variety of curious objects.

The fireplace, for instance, was adorned with a finely carved mantle from New Orleans and a silver tea set from Boston. On the wall above those fineries hung an old flintlock rifle. I figured that rifle had once killed opossum and other lowly beasts to feed a half-starved frontier family of an earlier generation of Kerns.

Next to that collection of treasures were the bookshelves. My eyes scanned the titles. There were some collections of poetry by Lord Byron. I was familiar with these because I had to read them for school. I snickered when I imagined Grandpappy Kern sitting around a campfire, eating opossum and reading Lord Byron.

There were also several Sir Walter Scott novels. My father had made me read some of these too, especially since Sir Walter Scott was a Scotsman like us. I actually liked *Ivanhoe.* It was a novel about the Middle Ages. In that story, all of the knights that were the "good guys" had chivalry, which was a fancy word for "honor." They always respected women, and always fought by the rules of "fair play." The bad guys were despicable knights who had no sense of honor. I remembered how my father said that these "good knights" were sort of heroes to the plantation owners like James Kern. I tried to imagine ol' Jamesie Kern in a suit of armor. I couldn't resist plopping down in one of the big arm chairs and sketching some of the pictures that flashed in my mind.

Before too long, the party started winding down. The fiddle player was packing up and the Kerns were saying goodbye to all of their guests with the same ceremony as they had greeted them. The tired faces of all the frontier folk had grateful looks as they said their "thank you's."

Just as my father and I were preparing to leave, Mr. Kern pulled us aside and said, "Angus, my friend, I must not let you leave without settling my payment for your work on the house. If you can tarry just a wee bit longer by the pasture gate, I'll meet you there."

My father was glad to do so. As we waited at the gate under the moonlight, I know we were both thinking that James Kern intended to pay us with one of his fine mares. We just knew that at any moment, Mr. Kern would come around the corner of the barn with a fine-looking horse. We discussed which one it might be, having admired them on many occasions. But, when Mr. Kern did join us at the gate, he was empty-handed and alone, except that his house servant Jethro had followed him. I was puzzled at the smile that beamed from Mr. Kern's face and even more confused to notice that Jethro was carrying a small bundle, like he was going on a trip.

"Angus, I cannot tell you how pleased I am with our fine new house," gushed Mr. Kern. "I am so proud of it that I had great difficulty in deciding how to pay you properly for your work. I thought about giving you one of my best horses, but you have horses already." At this point my heart fell, and I know my father's did too. Mr. Kern continued, "I wanted to pay you with something you did not have. Something that would make you a true gentleman. For those reasons, I am proud to present to you my faithful servant, Jethro." It was obvious by looking at his face that Mr. Kern felt he was bestowing a great gift on us. My father was stunned.

"I don't know quite what to say . . ." my father stammered. We both looked at Jethro. He appeared to be

unfeeling as he stared at the ground, but he must have felt like an orphan being given away to strangers. I felt awful for him.

"Now, Angus, I know your home is not very large, but your business is growing, and Jethro will be a great help in managing your affairs and entertaining clients. Maybe you can fix up that old dog-trot cabin on your back pasture for Jethro until the time comes that you build a larger home."

Mr. Kern stopped talking and was obviously waiting for Angus' response. I knew that my father was probably reeling inside. But to turn down Jethro would have been an insult to Mr. Kern. It would also have revealed that my father was not comfortable with the whole idea of slavery, which would have put him at odds with all of his clients. So in the end, all my father could say to James Kern was "Thank you."

We gave Jethro my horse, and the two of us climbed onto my father's. We waved to Mr. Kern and headed down the road, with Jethro silently following. Several times I saw Jethro look back as we left the Kern Plantation. I know it must have been hard. He'd probably been born there and rarely ever been off of the plantation except maybe for a trip to town.

The three of us did not utter a word for the first couple of miles. I tried to break the ice by jokingly calling my father "Master McBride." He gave me such an icy glare in return that I decided it wasn't very funny.

Chapter 4

Stuck in a Dog-Trot

The moonlit night had changed. A thunderstorm had blown in, and forks of lightning were arching from cloud to cloud above us. We rode a little faster, trying to reach home before the rain really cut loose. By the time we reached our back pasture, we were all soaked to the skin.

"Let's make for the old cabin, until the rain slows," my father yelled over the storm. We veered off the road through some trees. It was very dark, but with a flash or two of lightning I could make out the profile of that old dog-trot cabin at the edge of the pasture. After being in the Kerns' home, this cabin hardly looked fit for humans. Its look was rough-hewn and homemade, but the truth was that three-quarters of the folks in Texas lived in "dog-trots" just like this one. This one, though, hadn't been lived in by anyone but raccoons for at least twenty years.

One thing about a dog-trot is they always have a covered porch. That's where we tied up the horses so they'd be out of the rain. Then Jethro and I shook water off of ourselves like a couple of hound dogs while my father fumbled around inside the dark cabin.

"Look out for varmints!" I hollered. In a few seconds, he had a lamp lit and we stepped inside to join him.

"That didn't take you long," I complimented my father. "It's like you live here or something, " I joked, still trying to change the somber mood of our threesome.

"I did live here . . . once," returned my father as he gazed at the old plank roof that, to our delight, was only leaking in a few places.

I had sort of forgotten that this was the cabin my father grew up in.

"Well, we'd better stick here 'til this storm lets up," announced my father. "We don't want ol' Jethro here catching pneumonia."

My father's awkward attempt at a joke only got a polite nod out of our new servant. Jethro then busied himself dusting off a few chairs for us to sit on, and building a fire in the fireplace. Without me asking, my father began to explain, "When your grandpa and me moved out of this shack to our new house I was about your age. He said at that time we should leave the place just as we had lived in it, so we could come visit it and remember our family's humble roots."

As I looked about the cabin, I had to agree. It was plenty humble. The cracks between the logs that formed the walls were big enough for light from the lightning to flash through. The plank roof was just high enough for a good-sized man to stand up in. The floor was hard, packed dirt and the fireplace was made of a "waddle," or sticks and mud. The furniture of the main room (and by the way, there were only two rooms) was a collection of wooden crates and homemade chairs. But the chairs had been fancied-up by stuffing cotton seed sacks with grass to make cushions.

"Didn't the place get hot with no windows?" I asked.

"You better believe it," he agreed, "but, we were too afraid of Comanches to have windows. Our plan was to board up the door when Comanches attacked, and shoot at them through the gaps in the log walls. But it didn't do no good. Comanches never came when you expected them to. They carried off your grandma and my sister while all the men were off hunting . . . Never heard from them again."

A long silence gave me a chance to notice that Jethro had built us a nice fire in the fireplace and was sitting very still and erect, listening to our conversation. Each of us had managed to find a place to sit where the roof didn't leak. Outside, the storm kept on crashing with fury.

I looked about the room we were in and tried to imagine my grandfather and his young family living there. The hardest part was to imagine my father as a young lad.

"What made Grandpa leave Scotland and come to a place like Texas?" I asked.

My father chuckled to himself and picked up a stick to whittle. He whistled while he thought about my question for a few seconds, then said, "You mean . . . what makes a man leave his homeland and move his loved ones thousands of miles, to a country where he may have to fight Comanches on his left, and Santa Anna on

91

his right, maybe even at the same time? What makes him leave his homeland, traditions, and all that is familiar to him, so he can live in a shanty like this?. . . Son, that's a mighty powerful question."

He paused to whittle again. "Yes, it's a mighty strong question. I'd wager our friend Jethro here could answer it for us."

Our eyes turned gently to our quiet guest. He looked back at us and politely smiled, but offered no answer.

"Well," my father continued, "I'll tell you how my father would answer that question. He would say that a man would take the risk of moving to Texas, with all of its dangers, because he wanted the right to starve." He stopped to see if I was taken aback by his odd statement. I am sure I was.

"Yes, sir," he continued. "He wanted the right to starve to death. He used to tell me we could have stayed in Europe, kept farming for that fat-rumped English lord and probably never gone hungry. But . . . we would never have had a chance to be really well-fed, either. Here, on the frontier, he had the chance to either eat like a king, or starve to death. He said he liked that. He liked the opportunity to be a success or a failure, to make his own mistakes, or to even fall flat on his face, just as long as he wasn't locked into mediocrity all of his life. I think he knew he might live his whole life in a dog-trot cabin like this. But I think he knew by coming to Texas, he'd at least have a chance to live in a mansion like Mr. Kern's."

Again there was a long silence except for the sound of rain on the roof.

"You like farming, Jethro?" my father asked, still trying to draw our new servant into conversation.

"No, sir, " came his short, polite answer. It caught me by surprise that he answered.

"Me, neither, Jethro, nor did my father. That's why I'm now an architect. I don't know if I'd had a choice if my old pappy hadn't decided to take some chances. Heck, I might decide next week that I want to be a doctor, and here, Tommy-boy could be . . . the undertaker."

We all laughed. Even Jethro. The ice was finally broken. Jethro even asked Angus some questions about our family. I had to wonder where Jethro's family was, but I was afraid to ask because I knew that he might not even know.

"You know, Tommy-boy," my father started in his philosophical tone, "I have often said that buildings, and houses, and such are sort of like symbols of people's dreams. What do you think the Kerns' house symbolizes?"

"You mean besides a pile of money," I snorted. "Well let me see . . . I'd say to the Kerns it symbolizes their family's rise to a comfortable living after fighting the frontier for two or three generations."

"Very good, my boy, very good," complimented my father. "Now, how about this place?" He motioned with his hand in a grand manner about the room.

Before answering, I looked at the dirt floor, the drafty walls, the old Comanche arrow still stuck in the roof beam. "I'd say . . . this old dog-trot symbolizes the price a person pays to take his own chances."

"I think you're right, laddie," my father said softly

and thoughtfully. "And I just can't get around that truth, that people crave that opportunity to take their own chances. At least the kind of folks that come to Texas. I believe it's the truth." Again, we listened to the storm whine and wail outside, while my father's words sank in.

"Jethro?" my father asked in a strange tone.

"Yes, sir?" was Jethro's dignified reply.

"What does Jesus say the truth can do for someone?"

"Sir," Jethro answered in a confident tone, "Jesus said the truth will make you free."

My father pulled his uncle's letter from his pocket and scanned it by firelight as the rain's rhythm continued to fill the air. He folded the letter with a smile, and stroked his chin for a second.

"Jethro, you're a fine fellow and I enjoy your company," he said, "but I got no more taste for being a master as I would for being a slave."

Jethro's usually serious and dignified face now showed some surprise at my father's strange statement. I wasn't sure if either of us knew what would come out of my father's mouth next.

"I figure you've never had much opportunity to take your own chances, but I think I've got an opportunity that would fit you like a glove."

My father paused to study Jethro for a second. Jethro squirmed a little.

"I have an uncle in Chicago whose hotel needs a gentleman who knows how to make fancy folks feel at home! I can think of no one being better for it than you.

You'd be earning a wage with no guarantees, but . . . you'd be a free man."

Angus and Jethro studied each other's face for a while. Finally, Jethro spoke. "I think I would like that opportunity mighty fine, Mr. McBride. I guess I'd like to take my chances too."

My father smiled his sly, Scottish grin and said, "Tommy-boy, let's get some tickets on the steamboat tomorrow. We're going for a little visit to Chicago."

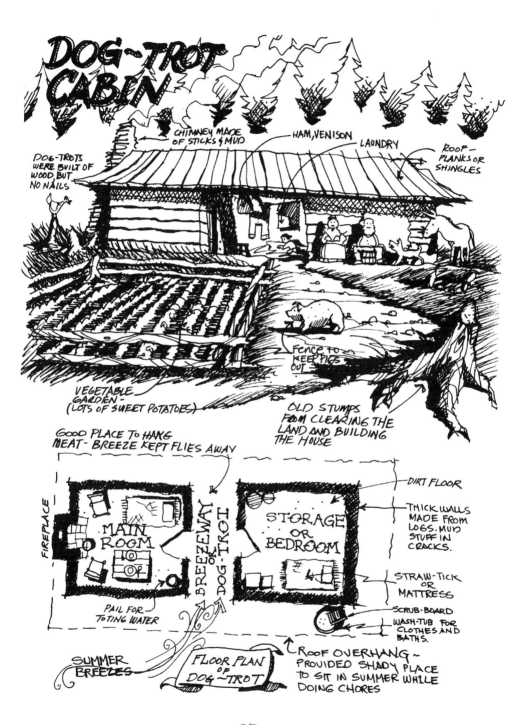

DOG-TROT CABIN

CHIMNEY MADE OF STICKS & MUD

HAM, VENISON

LAUNDRY

ROOF- PLANKS OR SHINGLES

DOG-TROTS WERE BUILT OF WOOD BUT NO NAILS

FENCE TO KEEP PIGS OUT

VEGETABLE GARDEN (LOTS OF SWEET POTATOES)

OLD STUMPS FROM CLEARING THE LAND AND BUILDING THE HOUSE

GOOD PLACE TO HANG MEAT - BREEZE KEPT FLIES AWAY

DIRT FLOOR

THICK WALLS MADE FROM LOGS. MUD STUFF IN CRACKS.

FIREPLACE

MAIN ROOM

BREEZEWAY OR DOG-TROT

STORAGE OR BEDROOM

STRAW-TICK OR MATTRESS

SCRUB-BOARD

WASH-TUB FOR CLOTHES AND BATHS.

PAIL FOR TOTING WATER

SUMMER BREEZES

FLOOR PLAN OF DOG-TROT

ROOF OVERHANG - PROVIDED SHADY PLACE TO SIT IN SUMMER WHILE DOING CHORES

About the Dog-Trot Cabin and Plantation Mansion

Many of the settlers who came to Texas in the 1800s were direct descendants of poor Scottish and Irish immigrants. Their families were those who came to this continent looking for something that they hadn't had in Europe — a chance to be prosperous. Because of their past, they were people who were willing to take chances, to live dangerous and difficult lives, if it meant something better might come to their children.

In this story, that's what the primitive dog-trot cabin represented. It represented the McBride family's willingness to take a chance in the frontier — no matter what the costs were.

The grand plantation mansion of the Kern family is a symbol too. It is a symbol of another Scotch-Irish family who had taken their chances on the frontier and had succeeded. The refined, sophisticated house showed they had fought the frontier and won. Culture and commerce had been established — but there were costs, in the form of slavery.

Crazy Water City

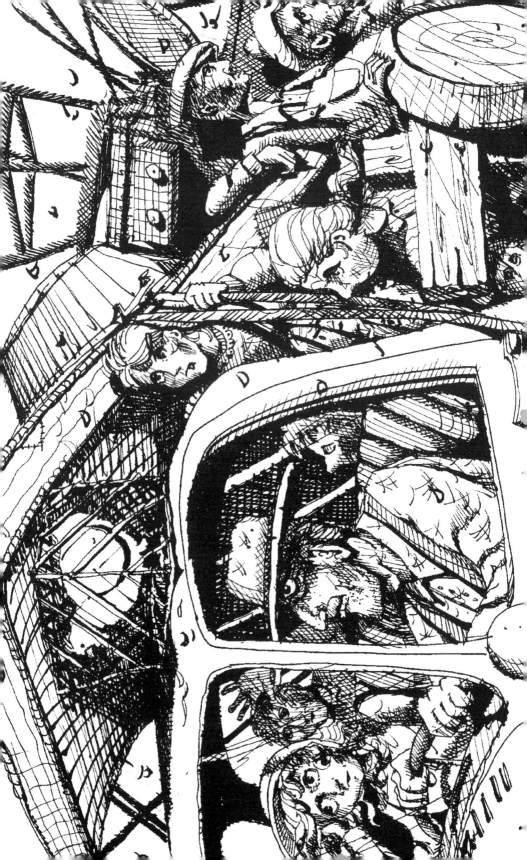

Chapter 1

Dirt Balls

I am still surprised we didn't just scare folks half to death. We must have been the dirtiest human beings you could imagine. Why, we could have been the "mud people from outer space" in a Flash Gordon movie! But these are the days of the Dust Bowl and the Depression in Texas, in the 1930s. And lots of families are flat broke. So seeing a pick-up truck full of furniture and filthy young-uns rumbling down the road is not too surprising. All a family like ours could do was load everybody and everything they owned into the truck and head out looking for a chance to start over.

After five years of drought, grasshoppers, and dust, Daddy finally gave up on our Panhandle farm. The papers called the drought the "Dust Bowl." Daddy called it "Death of a Dream."

"Gonna give up on the country life," he said. "We're gonna find some city jobs."

101

Yep, as I sat in the back of the truck trying to keep my dirty hair out of my face, it sure seemed like my Daddy had plenty of burdens to carry. He didn't have no money, no job, no house, and no way to feed Momma and seven kids. But as big as all those burdens seemed to be, I thought, Daddy's biggest burden was what to do with me. Because, you see, I'm twelve years old and my legs don't work no more. And for a girl who is supposed to grow up to be a farmer's wife, that's not good.

The back of a truck full of kids and junk is no place for a pity-party. So I did what I always did when I felt a "sad" coming on. I whistled.

We'd been rattling down long, lonely country high-ways since yesterday. The last time we stopped was several hours ago when Daddy stopped to shoot a deer from the highway. As soon as he had thrown the dead animal into the back of the truck, we were on our way. My little brother, Dab, thought it was a new toy.

Now I could see the dark county highway was leading us to a brightly lit city. A "Welcome to Mineral Wells" sign flashed past us. That was the last sign that made any sense to me. From then on, we were saluted by an army of signs that said stuff like "Crazy Water"; "Wonder Water!"; "Drink your way to health"; and "Soak with the Stars!" There were signs about rheumatism and insomnia. There were even signs asking me if I was constipated. Were we going to a city, or a hospital? I was really wondering what kind of city Daddy had brought us to.

It wasn't long until I found out. One minute we had the silent highway to ourselves, the next minute we were

102

in bumper-to-bumper traffic, surrounded by neon lights and honking horns, and fancy folks in shiny convertibles.

I don't guess any of us were too surprised that all of these city folk were staring at us.

"Are we still in Texas?" I asked one of my brothers.

"Of course we are, Bird!" he snapped.

I could tell that he thought that was about the dumbest question I had asked today.

"Everything just looks so different," I explained.

This city truly did look different. Every other town I had seen lately looked like it was well on its way to becoming a ghost town. They had all kind of looked the same. Sand dunes were climbing up the side of most of the buildings. Tumbleweeds were more plentiful than people. The dust was so thick on most of the shop windows that you could hardly read the "closed" signs.

But here in Mineral Wells, they hadn't seemed to have heard of the Depression or the Dust Bowl. The streets looked like one big party. Hotel signs boasted of dancing. Big Band music filled the air. Nicely dressed couples strolled down the street. I wasn't sure who was more decked out — the ladies in their fancy outfits or the modern buildings covered with doo-dads and gee-gaws. What on earth could make this city so prosperous? I wondered.

I felt the truck slow down to turn. Daddy was wheeling the truck into a gas station. We came to a stop in front of the gas pumps and a bell somewhere told the attendant he had customers. As I looked around me, I could hardly believe how fancy even the gas station was.

The light-up signs made me think a show was gonna start any second. Instead, only a bored-looking guy in a uniform sauntered to the driver's window.

"Fill'er-up?" he asked Daddy.

"Only five gallons," Daddy said. "Unless I can trade you some venison for a full tank?" he asked, motioning to the rear of the truck.

The attendant ambled back to the crowded bed of the pick-up. He kind of snickered at the collage of kids and rocking chairs and other keepsakes that were jumbled together. He saw the dead deer lying in one corner. Dab was asleep, using it for a pillow.

The attendant stroked the deer's hide and asked Daddy, "How long has it been dead?"

"Oh, about six hours."

Their voices awoke Dab, and the whites of his eyes flickered open to contrast with his dusty face.

"Ooh . . . weee," the attendant chuckled. "Dust balls coming to life!"

I guess he thought that was funny. We didn't.

"Looks like the venison is gonna be supper for you folks, but I will swap you the hide for a tank of gas."

"It's a deal," Daddy said without hesitation. The attendant pumped the gas and tried in vain to wash the truck windows. Daddy promised to bring him the deer-hide tomorrow and then he asked one more question.

"Where's someplace to stay a few nights?"

"There's the two big hotels . . . the Baker and the Crazy," he said with a grin. I guess he thought that was funny too. Daddy just waved politely and drove away.

Well, families like us didn't have no money for any

of these fancy hotels, so Daddy just kept on driving, right through to the other side of that busy city. Just as the road was getting quiet again, a sign appeared:

Dr. Zeke's Wonder Wells
10 miles to the left
Help for the lame, Healing for the sick
Camping 25¢ per night

Daddy obeyed the sign and turned left on the gravel road. That's the last I remember before I fell asleep on my brother's dusty shoulder.

Chapter 2

Camping at Dr. Zeke's

My eyes flickered open and I took a deep breath of cool morning air. Sunlight was filtering through a sheet of canvas that hung over me, so I knew we were camped somewhere. "Oh yeah," I remembered, "we must be at that 'Dr. Zeke's' place."

I just lay there for a few minutes listening for familiar sounds. I could faintly pick out my brothers' and sisters' voices. It sounded like they were working at something. Probably helping Momma set up camp.

I used to hate doing chores for Momma. It was like she never ran out of things for me to fetch. But now, I couldn't do nothing because of my legs. If you can believe it, I actually missed doing chores with my brothers and sisters. And even worse, now everyone had to do chores for me.

Most days, everyone was real cheerful when they had to fetch me this or that. But some days, everyone

seemed to stomp around and grunt when they had to
do something for me. I hated those days. I guess I know
how Momma feels.

I started whistling a little song just to let them know I
was awake. Soon, I could hear Momma's feet crunching
through grass toward my tent. In a second, her alert face
poked through the tent flap and smiled down at me.

"You awake?" she clucked cheerfully.

"Yes'm, I think," was my sleepy reply. She crawled
into the tent next to me and found the cotton dress that
I had been wearing for a week. I sat up and watched her
lovingly shake off the dust from it. She slipped the dress
over my head and combed my hair with her busy

fingers. It had been nearly a year since my legs quit working, but I still wasn't used to having Momma dress me.

Having got my top half ready for the day, Momma pulled back my blanket. She looked at my lifeless legs a second and pursed her lips. Then she glanced at my face and her mouth changed to one of her encouraging smiles.

"Are you hungry?" she chirped, as she lifted one of my legs to slip on a sock and shoe. I nodded.

"Well, while you're down at the well, I'll get some bacon on the fire."

"Down at the well?" I asked.

"Yep . . . your Daddy wants you to soak your pitiful little legs in these mineral springs at least an hour a day."

I must have looked bewildered.

"Now, Birdy, you know that's the main reason we came to Mineral Wells. Your Daddy is sure this crazy water will bring your legs back to life."

"I thought that we came here for jobs," I whispered, "and 'cause our farm was turned to dust."

"Well . . . that too," Momma replied.

My dressing was now complete, so Momma called for my oldest brother, Bobby, to come carry me to the springs.

Bobby's big, strong farm boy arms scooped me up and lifted me from the tent into the morning air. I gazed about at the makeshift camp my family must have set up last night while I slept. Not too far away other families and other camps were sprinkled among the trees. I wondered if they had lost their farms, too, or had someone like me in need of healing.

Bobby carried me past our campfire where my other brothers and sisters scurried about helping Momma. To see all of them working together while I was so useless always gave my stomach a yank. They each told me "Good mornin'" as Bobby toted me down a little trail through the trees.

The trail led to a little pool of water about the size of a baseball diamond. A wooden sign stood by proclaiming:

Dr. Zeke's Wonder Well
Hundreds cured!
All the water you want
25¢ a Day

Since an odd-looking fellow sat on a large rock on one side of the pool, Bobby carried me around to the opposite side. There were some steps leading into the water. As gently as he could, he lowered me onto a small stone seat. After taking off my socks and shoes, he eased my legs into the water. The water was cold!

"You sit there and get a good soaking," Bobby ordered in his big brother voice.

Like I could jump up and run off, I thought to myself. I just nodded, and he strolled around in the nearby trees, tossing rocks.

There was nothing to do but sit there and stare at my motionless legs. How strange life had gotten. I started whistling a tune from church which reminded me to pray for Daddy to find a job.

Chapter 3

The Big Hotel

Well, this routine went on for several days. We lived at our camp at Dr. Zeke's. I soaked my legs every day, and Daddy went to town to look for work. Jobs were hard to come by because of the Depression, so we weren't surprised each night that Daddy came home with no good news.

I liked sitting around the campfire at night the best. We'd take turns telling stories, and Daddy held us spellbound with his tales from town. I really wanted to see some of the things he described. He talked about movie theaters and street cars, and cafes, and beauty parlors, and all kinds of other stores.

After we all got talked out, we'd turn the radio on in the truck. Then we'd all sit back and look at the stars and listen to Big Band music broadcast from one of the hotels in town. This "Big Band Sound" was kind of new music, so us kids ate it up. It was sort of like jazz, but

111

with a lot more instruments. I think Momma preferred the country music of a group called the Light Crust Doughboys. What a name!

One day, Daddy came back from town wearing an ear-to-ear smile. He didn't have to tell us. We knew he'd found a job! Everyone listened as he told us that he was going to be a waiter in one of the fancy hotels in town. He said with the tips he'd make from all the "big shots" staying there, he should make a lot more money than one of those government work programs would pay.

"And another thing," he said, "they've got the healingest spring water in the whole city, and they said I can bring Birdy with me to soak her legs!"

Oh, he looked so hopeful when he said that, it nearly broke my heart. I would go, but I just had a feeling we'd both be disappointed.

I was so excited when I found out Daddy had gotten a city job. It meant food to eat, clothes to wear, and maybe even someplace to live.

But that first day I went to town with Daddy, my heart sank. Here was a man I was used to seeing perched proudly on top of a tractor. He had been a warrior, battling the weather and the seasons to take care of his crops. To me, he was made for the outdoors. Now, in his new city job, he seemed awkward and clumsy in a waiter's apron and bow tie. His weathered face and big hands looked out of place waiting on fancy folks at the hotel. His booming voice seemed to make questions like "Care for any cream?" sound pretty silly. But he worked real hard at his new job, and at being cheerful around the family.

One of the great things about going into the city with Daddy every day was that I had a chance to talk to him. You know, ask questions and such. That may not sound like a big deal to you, but with seven brothers and sisters it's tough getting a word in edgewise.

"Daddy, how does a city get started?"

He thought for a minute. "Jobs. It's all about jobs. A city's where people can find work like in a mine, or a seaport, or a factory."

"How about this one? How'd it get started?" I asked, gazing out the window. (I even got to sit in the front seat when it was just me with Daddy!)

"Well, this one got started because the spring water here is so good for your health. Folks from all over the country came here to drink it or soak in it. Just like you're doing, Birdy."

As far as going into town to soak my legs, I had my doubts. Up to now, all the soakings at Dr. Zeke's hadn't done anything but keep my feet clean. But the good thing was, I got to leave the campsite and see all the doings in town.

Being in a farm family all of my life, it seemed like all the folks I'd ever known had been farmers. Here in the city, there were all kinds of people doing all kinds of jobs — jobs I never knew even existed. There were guys that fixed cars, and guys that fixed breakfast. Some men scooped ice cream from a tub, and some scooped manure from the streets. There were some who sewed clothes and some who sold cars. And to my greatest delight, there were musicians — lots of them. They played in bands, in dance halls, and night clubs, and best of all, in the hotel.

113

In fact, that's what made soaking my legs at the hotel bearable. You see, at the hotel, they had indoor
plumbing. Healing water was pumped into this fancy
room with a huge bathtub in it. They called it "the spa."
Folks put on bathing suits and sat in it. That's where I
was every day.

The band that played in the hotel practiced in a
room next to the spa. So instead of being totally bored
watching my toes get wrinkled, I got to listen to all the
latest "swing" music. It was great!

Chapter 4

Swingers

One day, as I was soaking in the spa, something happened that changed everything. It's a good thing, too, because I had begun to think I was going to spend my whole life sitting in water watching my toes turn into prunes.

I was sitting there listening to the band practice and whistling along to the music. (You're probably getting an idea of why I'm called Birdy.) I heard footsteps pass the door going down the hall. That wasn't unusual because the hotel was busier than an ant hill. What *was* unusual is that I heard the footsteps stop suddenly, and then I heard the footsteps coming back to the door of the spa.

I stopped whistling. I was afraid there was some rule I had broken about whistling in the spa. The face that belonged to the footsteps peered in the door. It was a long, white face with stringy hair and a perfectly trimmed beard. It was not a face that been outdoors much. He smiled.

"Was that you whistling?" he asked in a funny accent.

"Yes, sir, I'm sorry if it was disturbing you," I apologized.

"No, no, not at all. It stopped me because you were whistling along with my band and hitting all of the right notes. Did you know you've got perfect pitch?"

"Uh, well . . . no," I stammered back.

"You're a musician, right?" he asked.

"Uh . . . no," I stammered again.

"Well, you oughta be. Hey, why don't you dry off and come watch us practice? We're really swinging!"

"Well . . . I can't . . . I can't walk," I said softly and awkwardly.

"Oh, geez . . . do I feel dumb." He looked at my legs and kind of frowned. It was his turn to feel embarrassed.

"What did it? Polio?" he asked.

"Yes, sir," I answered.

"Now I get it. You're Hank the waiter's daughter, aren't you? He was telling us about you."

I felt better about talking to him since he knew Daddy, and boy could he talk. We chatted about my family and the farm. He told me he was Stan, originally from New York, and a musician all of his life. Now he had his own band and was on a gig here for a couple of months.

"So what's the deal . . . you gotta sit here all day or something?" he asked.

"For an hour or so each day," I answered. "Daddy checks on me every once in awhile."

"You bored stiff?" he asked, nodding like he knew I was.

"Well, I would be if ya'll weren't next door practicing. I think I could sit here all day listening to music."

"Hey! I got an idea," he said. Stan disappeared for a second. When he returned he was carrying a leather case about the size of a large loaf of bread.

"My clarinet player ran off and got married and left this behind. No one else plays the clarinet, so why don't you give it a try? I mean, as long as you're just sitting here. You've got such a good ear, just play along with us."

I was delighted to have something to do, but it did seem a bit scary. Anyways, after he left, I opened up the case. There was a nice, shiny clarinet. We hadn't seen many Christmas presents the last few years, so I thought that clarinet was the most beautiful thing I'd ever seen.

Unfortunately, most of the sounds that I made with it were not quite so pretty. But I experimented, and over the next couple of days Stan and the other members of his band would stop in to show me some things. I became sort of the band mascot, and they all seemed to take pride in my progress. They were a funny group of folks, but I really liked them. It's kind of amazing how fast you can pick up something when you don't have any choice but to practice.

I wasn't sure what Daddy would say about my new friends and my new hobby. But when he saw how much it lifted my spirits, he seemed to be glad.

After several months of soaking my legs and playing my clarinet, Stan dropped in one day and remarked, "I thought you said you weren't a musician. You're doing great!"

"Well, I guess I've played the piano in church before. Does that count?" I asked.

117

"Hey! A lot of great musicians got their start in church," he said. "You know, Birdy," he started in a more serious tone that surprised me. "Me and the band, we've been giving you all these free music lessons and everything . . . Well, we think it's time for you to start paying us back." My heart sank. Did I owe them money or something?

"Yeah . . ." he went on, "we think it's time for you to pay us back . . . by joining the band."

I stared back at him. "You mean you want me to play in your band? Like when you perform at night and everyone dances and pays to get in? Stuff like that?" I stammered in amazement.

"Yeah . . . stuff like that," Stan grinned. "We think

you're good and we need someone to fill that clarinet chair. What do you say?"

"I gotta ask my folks, but I really want to," was my answer.

Back at camp that night, we all sat around the fire and talked about me joining the band.

"They must think you're pretty good," said Momma proudly.

"And you're gonna get paid for tooting that thing?" asked Dab innocently. We all chuckled.

"Yeah, a few cents a day is all, but it's more than I am making right now, which is nothing," I answered.

"Nothing" is probably all my family had thought I would ever do the rest of my life. By now, even Daddy had given up on me being healed. I think they had thought a farmer's daughter who couldn't walk didn't have many options. But here in the city, there were so many things a person could do. Everybody was real excited for me, even though I could tell they were still getting used to the idea. I was gonna get paid to play music!

Well, the next day, my Daddy carried me into the band's practice room. It would be the last time he had to carry me around. There, waiting for me in the band's practice room, was a homemade wheelchair.

Stan said, "What do you think? We wanted to get you a store-bought wheelchair, but the best we could do was make one from old bicycle parts. Hey, it's the Depression!"

Daddy set me in it, squeezed my hand, and walked away. It was a new day for me. It was a scary day. No more excuses for the lame girl. I had a job. I had a way to get around. Hey, I could even take myself to the restroom! The Lord had opened a door for me. I had to do all I could to step through it.

And I did my best. The band made me practice, practice, practice — and then practice some more. I learned all of the lingo, so I could throw around words like "jam" and "riff" and "square." I learned the differences between different styles of music, like jazz and bop and swing, which is what we played mostly. I could even quote famous musicians like Duke Ellington, who said, "It don't mean a thing, if it ain't got that swing."

With a wheelchair, I didn't have to be carried around anymore, so I got to know my way around town too. I guess I had an affection for the city, so I explored as much of it as I could in a wheelchair. Heck, I could have been a tour guide. I knew all the best places to get a hamburger, soda, or shake. I knew which movie theaters charged fifteen cents and which charged a quarter. I knew where to hang out to see some of the V.I.P.s (very important people) who came to town.

I always noticed the buildings. The ones I saw when we were farming were pretty basic. No frills. Just shelter. Here in town, buildings seemed to have personality. Some were decorated like a wedding cake. Some looked like spaceships. Stan called these buildings "Art Deco." He'd traveled a lot, so he knew these things. I told him that the decorations on Art Deco buildings kind of reminded me of what jazz or swing would look like, if you could see music.

The buildings that I thought looked like a wedding cake he said were "Spanish Mission" style. Stan said he hadn't ever seen any quite like them 'til he came to Texas. I thought they were pretty because they reminded me of classical music, like Bach and Beethoven. Stan said I was certainly observant.

Another thing I observed about buildings was that most of them were built for people with two good legs. I guess none of those architects who designed those building had to get around in a wheelchair. Tight doorways, stairways, narrow halls, high mirrors — all these things make it tough on someone like me. Let me tell you, it's really embarrassing to get stuck in a restroom because you can't get your wheelchair turned around.

Because of stuff like that I eventually "graduated" from the wheelchair to crutches. This made things a little easier.

Well, all my sightseeing and getting to know the town really started me to thinking. One afternoon after practice, Stan and I were grabbing a drink at one of the soda parlors.

"Stan?" I asked.

"Yeah, Birdy," he replied.

"You've been around. How does a town like this spring up out of nowhere when everything else around it is dying on the vine?"

"Dreams, Birdy, dreams," was his smooth reply. "Dreams of jobs, dreams of excitement. In this case, dreams of good health built this city with all of its night life and hustle and bustle."

"You mean these big hotels were built so folks from all over the country could come here and drink this crazy water in hopes of getting better from whatever ails them?" I asked in mild surprise.

"Well . . . yeah . . ." was Stan's answer. "Look, I've been around. Buildings get built for some pretty crazy dreams. Having better health is not so crazy. Don't you believe folks should dream of getting better?" Stan asked.

"Sure," I replied. Then I changed my voice to a whisper. "But do you really believe this water will do anything?"

"You tell me," Stan shot back. "You're the one who's been sitting in it every day for almost a year. Do you think it's helping your legs get any better?"

"No," I said, and shook my head.

"Does that make you sad?" Stan asked gently.

"No, not anymore," I answered. "I've gotten used to the idea that I'm going to carry my legs around like a couple of empty suitcases the rest of my life. I'm just so afraid that my Daddy is disappointed. He told me when I first got polio that he was still gonna plan to dance with me at my wedding someday. I don't guess there's much chance of either of those things happening."

"Well," said Stan, "if you can't dance to music, I'll bet he's just as proud to hear you making music."

After that day, I didn't bother to soak my legs anymore. To my surprise, no one in my family asked me about it. With that time freed up, I could spend more time practicing on my music. I had been performing nearly every night with the band and having a great time. Every night, folks in their fanciest clothes would fill up the ballroom where we played. They would eat dinner, dance to our music, and applaud every song. I never got tired of it.

No one in my family but Daddy had ever heard me perform. My brothers had found jobs that kept them busy, and someone had to stay at the camp all of the time with Dab. But now that we'd all been working and pooling our money together, we had enough to get a little house in town. It was at a cheap price because of the Depression and all. After sleeping under canvas and washing my face in a bucket for a year, I'd almost forgot how to live in a house.

On the first night we moved in to our new place, Daddy made an announcement.

"Tonight, we're gonna do something special," he

said proudly. "We're all going down to hear Birdy perform at the hotel."

A night out for the whole family! You never saw so much excitement and frenzy as everyone got slicked up. Since I had to get to the hotel early to rehearse, I caught the street car.

It seemed like any other night. I warmed up with the band in the back room. We changed into our band outfits, and when we heard the hotel manager announce us, we took the stage. I crutched my way to my chair as gracefully as I could.

And sure enough, when I looked out at the audience, there was my family. All of their tanned farmer faces crowded eagerly around a table draped with white linen. Their eyes were big. Their smiles were wide. They looked like they were proud of me. But I was really proud of them. We weren't farmers anymore. In a way that was sad, but our lives had been forced to change and we had made that change. That was something to be proud of. I played my best for them that night and every night after that, whether they were there or not.

Stan and I were chatting over a soda at the drug store one day.

"Well, Birdy, you are an accomplished musician now with a growing reputation," Stan remarked. "Did you ever imagine this was your future when you were sitting around soaking your legs all day?"

"No, I would never have guessed this is where I'd be today. I thank the Lord for bringing you along to be my teacher," I replied.

Stan blushed a little. "Well, it only took the Depression, the Dust Bowl, and polio to bring you to the city. Otherwise, I never would have met you."

"Yeah, the city's a good place for someone like me," I stated.

"How's that, Birdy?" Stan asked.

"Well, farm life is a good life, but it only offers opportunities to folks with strong arms and legs. The city offers more to more kinds of folks," I said philosophically. "Texas will always be known for farmers and ranchers, but I'm betting more and more Texans will wind up being city folks."

ART DECO

ART DECO BUILDING LOOKED LIKE MACHINES, OR SPACE SHIPS

METAL ORNAMENT

VERTICAL EMPHASIS

FLASHY SIGNS

MOVIES

SYMBOLS OF BUSINESS BECAME BUILDING DECORATIONS

ART DECO WAS THE MODERN LOOK IN THE 1930's, IT WAS VERY POPULAR FOR MOVIE THEATERS AND RETAIL STORES

SPANISH COLONIAL WAS A POPULAR STYLE FOR GOVERNMENT & EDUCATION BUILDINGS

CLAY TILE ROOFS

SPANISH COLONIAL REMINDS YOU OF A CASTLE FROM THE MIDDLE AGES

LOTS OF SYMMETRY

ARCHES

COLUMNS OR PILASTERS

About Architecture
of the 1930s

In this final story a fourth Texas home is discussed. This fourth home is the "city."

In the early twentieth century, more and more Texans left the rural life and became city-dwellers. This migration to the city from the country increased in the 1930s. Driven by the Depression and changes in farming methods, people moved to cities looking for jobs.

One of the most unique Texas cities of the early 1900s was Mineral Wells. People from all over America traveled to Mineral Wells hoping the city's natural spring water would cure their ailments. There they would have been greeted by two popular styles of architecture. One style, Spanish Colonial, was based on the Spanish missions of early Texas. These buildings were highly decorated and had an "old world" charm. The "Art Deco" building sort of looked like a machine or space-ship, and was considered to be the look of the modern age. It seems fitting that two styles — one based on the past, and one looking to the future — would greet Texans as they left their country roots.